Sharon swam the length of the pool, back and forth until her body was tired. Then she retreated to the side of the pool to watch Conall slice through the water with power and grace. . . .

He'd always  now his power wa... ...ned to cool elegan... ...nst the pool's edg... ...he was still the m... ...et.

Suddenly Co... ...urse and headed toward her. When he stopped, he had trapped her against the wall with a hand on either side of her head. Her heart pounded rapidly but it was not from the exertion of her swim. Instead, without even touching her, Conall was affecting her physically, leaving her breathless. Before she could say a word, he leaned over and pressed a deep kiss to her mouth. Her body responded instantly, and her lips parted of their own volition, no matter that she'd planned to resist.

"Did the swim release some of that tension?" he asked.

She nodded. "I had to stop, though. I'm not in as good shape as you are."

He brushed his hands down the sides of her body. "There's nothing wrong with the shape you're in. In fact, I find it quite alluring."

"You shouldn't do this," she said quickly. "Someone might come in."

"I locked the door of the pool house," he answered, caressing her gently. "We can do anything we want here and no one will interupt us. . . ."

WHAT ARE *LOVESWEPT* ROMANCES?

They are stories of true romance and touching emotion. We believe those two very important ingredients are constants in our highly sensual and very believable stories in the *LOVESWEPT* line. Our goal is to give you, the reader, stories of consistently high quality that may sometimes make you laugh, sometimes make you cry, but are always fresh and creative and contain many delightful surprises within their pages.

Most romance fans read an enormous number of books. Those they truly love, they keep. Others may be traded with friends and soon forgotten. We hope that each *LOVESWEPT* romance will be a treasure—a "keeper." We will always try to publish

LOVE STORIES YOU'LL NEVER FORGET
BY AUTHORS YOU'LL ALWAYS REMEMBER

The Editors

LOVESWEPT® • 419

Fayrene Preston
SwanSea Place: The Promise

BANTAM BOOKS
TORONTO • NEW YORK • LONDON • SYDNEY • AUCKLAND

THE PROMISE
A Bantam Book / August 1990

*LOVESWEPT® and the wave device are registered
trademarks of Bantam Books, a division of
Bantam Doubleday Dell Publishing Group, Inc.
Registered in U.S. Patent
and Trademark Office and elsewhere.*

*All rights reserved.
Copyright © 1990 by Fayrene Preston.
Cover art copyright © 1990 by Ralph Amatrudi.
No part of this book may be reproduced or transmitted
in any form or by any means, electronic or mechanical,
including photocopying, recording, or by any information
storage and retrieval system, without permission in
writing from the publisher.
For information address: Bantam Books*

If you would be interested in receiving protective vinyl covers for your Loveswept books, please write to this address for information:

> *Loveswept*
> *Bantam Books*
> *P. O. Box 985*
> *Hicksville, NY 11802*

ISBN 0-553-44049-7

Published simultaneously in the United States and Canada

---

*Bantam Books are published by Bantam Books, a division
of Bantam Doubleday Dell Publishing Group, Inc. Its trademark, consisting of the words "Bantam Books" and the
portrayal of a rooster, is Registered in U.S. Patent and
Trademark Office and in other countries. Marca Regis-
trada. Bantam Books, 666 Fifth Avenue, New York, New
York 10103*

PRINTED IN THE UNITED STATES OF AMERICA

OPM   0 9 8 7 6 5 4 3 2 1

Preface

The gray light of dawn seeped around the edges of the drapes and into Clarisse Haviland's bedroom. Standing by the bed, belting her rose velvet dressing gown, she frowned at the intruding light. She was not ready for the night to end. She had so few nights left with him. . . .

Jake Deverell stirred beneath the covers. She turned toward the sound and him.

"What are you doing up so early?" he asked huskily, rubbing the sleep from his cobalt-blue eyes.

"I woke up and couldn't go back to sleep."

"Why didn't you wake me?"

"Your last exam is today. I felt you needed your rest."

He groaned good-naturedly. "You sound like my mother."

She swung away, but not fast enough to keep him from seeing that he had hurt her. In a flash he was standing behind her, his big hands cupping her upper arms and drawing her back against him. "I'm sorry, Clarisse. I didn't mean that the way it sounded."

"I know."

He swept her long brown hair free of one shoulder and pressed his lips to the side of her neck.

A sweet warmth flooded through her. But then, he could always evoke a response from her with just the lightest of touches. She lay her head back against him and reached behind her to clasp his hips; muscles flexed beneath her hands, thrilling her.

"I've told you time and again, to me you are ageless," he whispered in her ear.

"To you," she said softly, "because you're gallant. But the truth is I'm thirty-four and you're twenty-two."

He turned her to face him. "Why are you bringing this up now, Clarisse? We've been together almost from the first day I arrived here to attend Harvard."

She smiled softly. "I remember. I glanced up and saw you staring in the window of my shop at the display of my latest hat designs. You looked so serious." And handsome, she added to herself. And tough. That day, something had moved inside her. Something that had felt like excitement and heat combined. Something that had never before moved in her, even when her husband had been alive.

"I was trying to decide which hat to buy for my mother. Then it occurred to me, I could buy them all."

Her smile widened. "Yes, and you did."

"And in doing so, I met you. I had just been through the biggest upheaval of my life, learning that Edward Deverell was my real father, then deciding whether or not to allow the bastard to adopt me—"

"Which you did, but only on your terms. You should be proud of yourself, Jake. You bested him."

He grinned affectionately. "Yes, and you have bested me by somehow managing to get me off the subject. Now answer me. Why are you bringing up the difference in our ages?"

"Because within a few days you will be graduating. SwanSea will become your home, and you will take your rightful place in society and begin your new life in earnest."

"Oh, I definitely intend to begin a new life. Unfortunately for Edward Deverell, it won't be the new life he's envisioning. He's given me the two things in the world he most cherishes: his name and his beloved SwanSea—not because of any love he has for me or my mother, but because he hopes I will make his dreams come true." His expression turned cruel. "In the coming years he will be dealt more disappointments than he will be able to bear."

"And what about SwanSea?" she whispered, taken aback by his vehemence.

"SwanSea will never be my home. I view it only as a tool with which to hurt Edward Deverell."

"But they say it's majestic, beautiful."

He glanced down at her, saw her lovely face and her soft blue eyes that held such wisdom, and felt the tension drain from his body. She could always make him feel better. He hugged her, then with a smile set her away from him again. "It's nothing more than an oversized plaything, Clarisse. You and I can play there together."

She shook her head, her expression full of love and regret. "No, Jake. My life is here in Cambridge with my hat shop, and my home is this apartment above the shop. I may be lonely after you leave, but I'll be content."

"You won't be lonely," he said decisively. "If you won't come to see me, I will come to see you.

SwanSea is only in the next state, and I imagine I'll be in Boston frequently."

"You say you will come, but—"

He let out an impatient sound and turned away from her. "I can't believe this rotten mood you're in." With the nonchalant grace and power of youth, he strode to the window and jerked back the drapes. The dawn's pale light poured over him, following the long lines of his bronze body, delineating the strong, supple muscles and the taut, corded sinews. Suddenly he snapped his fingers. "I know what I'll do! I'll *give* you something. Anything. Name it. What do you want?"

She laughed. "Nothing. Absolutely nothing."

"But you've given me so much! I couldn't have made it through these last four years without you, and I insist on giving you a present. I know! I'll choose the present myself. Something wonderful, something—"

"I won't accept, Jake. I'm serious."

He stared at her, perplexed. "But why not?"

"Because no gift could be as wonderful as the time I've spent with you. You think I've given you so much? It's not half what you have given me. The memory of you will stay with me the rest of my life."

"You're being foolish, Clarisse." He made an abrupt gesture that was uniquely his and that conveyed the life and energy in him that was ready to explode. "Never mind. I know what I will do."

He strode to her desk, sat down, and drew pen and paper from a drawer. Magnificent in his nakedness, he began to write in sweeping, broad strokes.

She watched him. Perhaps it was the light, she thought. Perhaps it was the moment. But it seemed to her she could see through to his inner self with absolute clarity—the good in him, the faults, the tremendous potential.

He was so very sure of himself. He thought he'd learned everything there was to learn, but he hadn't. He thought he had the world tamed and that all the rough times were behind him, but there would be more. He thought he was everything he could be now, but it was nothing compared to what he would become.

A thought occurred to her. Jake would have extraordinary children, and she envied the woman who would bear them.

He finished with a flourish, stood, and handed her the paper.

She bent her head and read.

I, Jacob Conall Deverell, hereby promise to grant a favor, unconditionally, to the bearer of this letter. In the event something prevents me from granting this favor, be it life or be it death, this promise is hereby binding on my heirs.

So stated in this the year of nineteen hundred and twenty-two.

Jacob Conall Deverell

One

Conall Jacob Deverell finished reading the note, lifted his head, and pinned the young woman sitting in front of his desk with a hard gaze. "Are you trying to tell me that my grandfather wrote this note to your great-aunt, Clarisse Haviland, and as a result I owe you a favor?"

Sharon Clarisse Graham inclined her head. "That's right."

"You've got to be kidding."

She glanced down at her clasped hands. "Your grandfather, in effect, wrote my great-aunt a promissory note."

"*If* Jake wrote this—"

"I assure you he did, but we can have an expert analyze the handwriting if you wish."

His expression turned flinty at her interruption. "—and *if* it was his wish to grant your great-aunt a favor, then it was to your great-aunt that the favor should have gone. The note says nothing about her heirs."

"What the note says is that the promise is binding on *his* heirs and that the favor is to be granted to the *bearer* of the note."

That was what it said all right, Conall agreed

silently, knowing under any other circumstances he would have been amused at the grandiose gesture his grandfather had made as a young man. Jake, at twenty-two, must have been really something, and Clarisse, quite a woman.

Nylon whispered against nylon. Clarisse's great-niece crossed her legs, breaking into his thoughts to remind him that she was a woman to be reckoned with as well, though in quite another way. But he was an accomplished gamesplayer in the world of business. He could handle her, though first he had to know what game they were playing and why they were playing it.

He had last seen her ten years before. She had never once in the intervening years tried to see him until today. She wanted money, of course.

"Your reputation in business is one of integrity," she was saying. "It is that integrity I'm counting on when it comes to the honoring of your grandfather's note."

"You're counting on a great deal."

"Oh, I'm well aware of that."

The mockery he saw in her greenish-blue eyes pricked at him. Slowly he closed his hand around the note, crushing it.

"It's a copy," she said softly.

"I don't care if it's an ancient piece of parchment found in the same cave with the Dead Sea Scrolls. There will be no favor granted to you."

She gave a patient sigh and settled more comfortably into the large wing chair. "All right, so much for honor. But what about your family's name?"

He took her quietly posed question as a threat. With his uncle, Senator Seldon Deverell, in the race for the presidency of the United States, he had to proceed carefully until he knew what she was up to. Reporters were nipping like hungry dogs for juicy tidbits on the Deverell family.

He dropped the crumpled note onto the desk and sat back in his chair to study her. When he'd known her, she'd been eighteen, her hair wildly curly, and a free, natural spirit. Now her light brown hair was straight, pulled away from her face, and held at her nape by a plain gold barrette. Light, deftly applied makeup enhanced her smooth ivory complexion. Clear fingernail polish covered her short, manicured nails. She wore a severely tailored navy blue pinstripe suit and a plain white blouse. The hem of the straight skirt covered her knee, even with her sitting.

All in all, her appearance was very proper, he thought. Very professional. Very appropriate for making her way in what she no doubt saw as a man's world.

But her look also had another consequence. It was sexy as hell, understated to the point that it worked on a man's mind, making him wonder what she was hiding beneath the very plain exterior. He was sure she had carefully calculated the whole effect.

He was also sure she had figured to the penny the exorbitant sum of money she planned to try to extort from him.

He watched her hand idly rub the leather handle of her briefcase, an arrogant gesture that conveyed his scrutiny wasn't bothering her and that she was content to wait until he was through. Very, very cool.

The card she had presented him at their meeting had stated she was a certified public accountant for what he knew to be a prestigious accounting firm. Perhaps she wanted the money to start up her own business, or even to buy a partnership in an existing company. The thing was, he didn't care if she said she wanted it for an operation for her poor sainted mother. She wasn't going to get it.

"Since you feel the promise is binding on Jake's heirs, why didn't you go to one of his other heirs—my father, for instance, or my cousin, Caitlin, or even my uncle, Senator Deverell. You could have caused quite a commotion in my uncle's camp."

"It's not my intention to cause a commotion, and I chose you because you're the most appropriate person for what I want."

She wanted to cause a commotion all right, he reflected cynically, and he knew why she had chosen him. Among other things, with his father retired, Caitlin interested in other things, and Seldon in politics, the Deverell business empire was totally and completely under his control. She must want an enormous sum. "Did you know about the relationship between your great-aunt and my grandfather when we were seeing each other?"

"I didn't know about the note, but I did know Jake and Clarisse had been involved."

"Why didn't you mention it?"

Again her eyes mocked him. "When we were together, other things always seemed more important."

A muscle moved in his jaw. "How is it that your family has never tried to cash in on this favor before?"

"I can't speak for my family. Perhaps no one has ever needed it."

"But you do. Need a favor, I mean."

She moved, he couldn't say exactly how. But it was just enough to make him consider that she might not be as at ease as she seemed. "I prefer to think of it as collecting on a promise."

"How long have you had the note?"

"I inherited it last year. Clarisse never had children—in fact, she never remarried—so the note was handed through her younger sister to her daughter, who was my mother, who in turn passed it on to me at her death."

"Is your father still living?"

"He died several years before my mother."

"I'm sorry." His jaw tightened. Dammit. Why had he let himself become sidetracked by personal matters?

He thumped the note with his thumb and middle finger. The crumpled ball of paper shimmied, then stilled. "You know, don't you, that this note would never hold up in court?"

Her chin seemed to lift a notch. "It's a chance I'm willing to take."

She had to be bluffing. She had to know that if she somehow managed to get him into court, a highly unlikely event, he could completely destroy her character.

"Your grandfather was a great man," she said. "I can't imagine you would want his name dragged through court."

"Yours would be there, too, right alongside his."

"And so would yours."

His eyes narrowed. "You must want this very badly."

There was another movement; this time he saw one of her fingers jerk and pull the skin of the hand on which it lay. The gesture bothered him in a way he couldn't put into words.

"Yes," she said quietly, "I do."

He'd had enough. He leaned forward, intense, predatory. "All right, let's quit playing games. I'll bite. How much do you want?"

For a moment she looked startled. "How much?"

He made a sound of impatience. "How much money do you want?"

"I don't want any money from you." Her derisive tone denounced him for jumping to that conclusion.

He blinked. "Then just exactly what is this favor you want?"

"I want you to make me pregnant."

He stared at her for a long moment. "I beg your pardon?"

"I want you to make me pregnant," she repeated, softer this time, but just as firmly.

He felt like a wall of bricks had fallen on him. Very slowly he leaned back in his chair.

Sharon eyed him warily, waiting for the explosion to come. When it didn't, she decided that his calm, awful control was in many ways more terrible than the explosion she had anticipated. "Do you mind if I pull this chair closer to your desk?" she asked rhetorically, already standing and gripping the arms of the mahogany and leather chair. "I have several documents to show you."

Conall watched her inch the heavy chair across the thick carpet, knowing he should help her but badly needing the time to think. At thirty-two years of age, he had assumed he had reached the state where he couldn't be shocked. He had assumed wrong.

Her request was preposterous! What in the hell did she hope to gain by it? By trying to hold him to this stupid promise, did she hope to embarrass him and the family? And if so, why?

He suddenly noticed the modest slit at the hem of her navy skirt, and the small amount of ivory lace that peeped out. His brows drew together in a scowl. So there was lace beneath the proper appearance, delicate, feminine lace. The idea disturbed him.

Satisfied now with the chair's position, Sharon sat down and pulled from her briefcase a sheaf of papers, a pair of brownish-red-framed glasses, and a pen. She laid the papers on the gleaming mahogany surface of his desk and donned the glasses.

"Now," she said as she handed him several clipped-together sheets of paper, "I have taken the liberty of having an agreement drawn up that I hope you will find satisfactory."

He dropped the document in front of him without even looking at it.

She felt his hard cobalt-blue gaze on her and tried not to let herself become rattled. She had known before she had come here today that he was a force, a power. And she had known that his masculine good looks were enough to stop a woman's heart. None of it was unexpected, she told herself, and she could cope. She just had to stick to her plan and keep this on a business level.

"The document outlines our individual responsibilities in this matter, and it is fairly simple. The sum total of your responsibility will be to impregnate me. All other responsibilities are mine. Upon signing this document, you will give up all claims and rights to the child, and, of course, the child will bear my last name, not yours." She glanced up at him.

"Are you out of your mind?" he asked quietly.

She started and her hand hit a Baccarat crystal swan paperweight, sending it skittering. His quick reflexes saved it from toppling off the side of the desk.

"Perhaps I should show you the chart first," she murmured, and lay another paper on top of the document already in front of him. His gaze never once wavered from her.

She lightly cleared her throat. "This chart documents my menstrual cycles for the last ten months. As you can see, I don't have a very regular cycle, which makes it somewhat difficult to plan the right time to conceive. But I have just finished my period, and I calculate that I should begin to ovulate in approximately one week." She tapped the end of her pen on her copy of the chart. "That week and the following one would be the time when I could conceive."

"What are you trying to do?" he asked. *And what are you trying to do to me?* he added silently.

"I'm trying to have a baby," she said.

"Try artificial insemination."

She shook her head. "It won't do for my purposes."

"This is pointless and you know it."

"No, I don't know it. All I'm asking is a small investment of your time over a two-week period."

He rubbed his forehead. He had had many propositions from women in his life, but hers was not only unexpected, it didn't make sense. And her answers to his questions were giving him no explanation, no hint as to what lay beneath this outrageous request of hers.

"Two weeks," he murmured thoughtfully, deciding to play along with her, at least for a few minutes. "As I understand conception, it would also require quite another sort of investment on my part."

She felt heat wash up her neck and saw his eyes follow the color.

"What is it you really want?"

"I've told you," she began, then stopped and drew a measured breath. "Perhaps if we look again at the legal agreement, you'll be able to understand that all I want from you is to make me pregnant. If you will refer to page two, paragraph four of the agreement, you will see that I will not now, or ever, request any money from you." She brought out more papers from the briefcase and held them up to him. "And these are my tax statements for the last five years that will verify to you that I am capable of supporting myself and my child without help from you."

She laid the tax statements on top of the still-unread chart and legal agreement. "I want you to be assured that the child will be well taken care of."

He got up, circled the desk, and perched on its corner.

She couldn't tell what he was thinking, but his nearness had caused a pressure in the air that seemed to touch her skin in an almost hurtful way. Thankful that she would soon be through, she continued on. "To further assure you that the baby's well-being is and will continue to be my top priority, I will tell you that in preparing for this baby, I have had no alcohol or any type of drug in the last ten months."

"Ten months. Since you've had the note a year, that means it took you two months to decide to ask me for this favor."

"That's right, and I assure you I didn't make the decision lightly." She reached for the final set of papers she intended to show him. "This is the result of my latest physical with attached blood tests that proclaim me free of all disease, communicable or otherwise. It also states, by the way, that I am not already pregnant." She paused while she added the tests to his growing stack of documents. "Of course, I will expect you to have the same tests done. Since you don't seem to engage in random sexual liaisons—"

"Don't seem to?" he asked, cutting in sharply.

She met his gaze coolly. "Don't worry. I haven't had you investigated. It wasn't necessary. All I had to do was keep up with the society columns. Those same columns also informed me that you are not currently involved with anyone. It makes it convenient all the way around."

His teeth came together with a snap. "I think it's time this interview ended."

"Perhaps you're right. I've covered everything I need to for the time being." She carefully folded her glasses away in the recesses of the briefcase and stood. "I'll leave these papers with you. Shall we say forty-eight hours for you to consider?" Turning for the door, she added, "My phone number is on my card."

He slipped his hands into his trouser pockets, the control he used completely unnecessary to the act. When she had almost reached the door, he said, "Actually, there is one more thing I would like to ask."

She turned and looked at him. "Yes?"

"Why me, Sharon? Why do you want *me* to try and make you pregnant?"

"Because, Conall, this time you'll know without a doubt that the baby is yours."

Sharon closed the door of her apartment behind her and eyed the distance between her and the couch that sat against one wall of her small living room. It appeared an incredibly long way for her to walk. Her steps were leaden, her legs weak. It seemed to take her an eternity to cross the room, and when at last she collapsed onto the couch, she let out an exclamation of relief.

She felt icy from head to toe and was shaking uncontrollably. The trembling had started as she left the Deverell Building and had grown progressively worse on the drive home.

Ten months had given her plenty of time to plan what would happen when she came face-to-face with Conall Deverell, but truthfully, ten years of careful preparation wouldn't have made today any easier. Walking into his imposing wood-paneled office—the seat of the Deverell power and the throne room of their crown prince—had taken every ounce of courage she possessed. And that had been only the beginning of the ordeal.

Conall had recognized her immediately; she hadn't been sure he would. It seemed to her she had grown and changed to the point that *she* might not even recognize the eighteen-year-old she had been when they had known each other. All she remembered of herself at that age was how tender her heart had been, how full of hope. And how he had broken it.

She tugged a crocheted afghan off the back of the couch and wrapped it tightly around her. She had to get warm; she had to stop shaking.

She was doing the right thing, she assured herself as she had many times before. The first part, possibly the worst part, was over, and she had done well.

She had remained self-possessed and dispassionate and had presented the matter to him in a businesslike manner. In the process, she had managed to surprise, shock, and stun him, just as she had hoped. Catching him off guard had been the only way she could think of to guarantee he would listen to her. She had even managed to get in the last word.

She pulled the afghan more closely around her. Of course, everything she had put herself through would be for nothing if he didn't agree to honor the promise. But she was counting on his pride and his ego, and she didn't think she would be disappointed.

The phone began to ring, then her answering machine switched on, and she heard his voice.

He gave the name and address of a restaurant, then said, "meet me there tonight at seven-thirty for dinner. If the place isn't to your liking, call me back and tell me where you would rather meet. But I think I deserve an explanation, don't you?"

The line went dead. Her machine turned off. A faint smile touched her lips.

She was over one more hurdle.

A vein pounded in Conall's temple as he stared at the phone he had just hung up. He had chosen a restaurant for their meeting in the hope that it would provide neutral surroundings for a calm, objective discussion.

Except he didn't feel the least bit calm and objective. Nor did he want to wait until this evening to see her again. He wanted her here now! He wanted to grab her and yell *What in the hell do you mean, this time I'll know for sure the baby is mine?*

He pressed a finger against the pounding vein. How dare she waltz into his office after ten years with that damned note of Jake's and demand *anything* of him, much less that he make her pregnant.

She knew better. She knew he couldn't make her or anyone pregnant. She knew he was sterile.

Conall watched the way the full skirt of Sharon's azure blue dress gently swayed back and forth with the movement of her hips as she walked ahead of him, following the waiter through the restaurant. The dress was as demure as the suit she had worn to his office, but less severe, softer, more interesting, relying as it did on a simple cut for its style and the wide shawl collar to offer a becoming frame for her face.

His anger had died down. He felt keyed up and tense, the same way he felt just before a good corporate fight. Battling any kind of adversary always made him feel a special kind of aliveness, and in this instance the fact that his adversary was Sharon made the upcoming fight all the more interesting.

Their table sat next to a wall of windows that overlooked the Charles River. Conall waved the waiter away and pulled out a chair for her. "Is this table all right?" he asked casually.

"It's fine," she murmured.

A cynical smile shaped his mouth. Although this was one of the best restaurants in the city, he was sure she would have met him anywhere. The damned promise aside, she wanted something from him, something other than what she had already indicated, and that made *him* the one in control.

As she took her seat, the scent of her unexpectedly rose through the air and circled him. It was a feminine, innocently seductive smell that rippled through his memory, teasing long-forgotten responses.

"Did you have any trouble finding this place?" he asked, deliberately moving away from her, rounding the table to his own chair, breaking the enticing chains of the fragrant, surprisingly threatening memories.

"I didn't drive. I took a cab, and the cab driver knew where it was."

"That was smart. Are you hungry? Would you care to order now or would you like to wait?"

She wasn't fooled by this polite, courteous act of his. The shock she had given him had obviously worn off, and she was in for a grueling evening. She just hoped she would be equal to it. "Later would be fine. For now I'd like a club soda."

"A club soda and a Scotch," he said to the waiter, then sat silently until the young man had left. "All right, Sharon, tell me truthfully what this is all about."

Her gaze was direct and unwavering. "I've already given you all pertinent information, and I made the situation as plain as I could this afternoon. As far as I'm concerned, all that's left is for you to give me your answer."

"Not quite all." He glanced over his shoulder to make sure no one was in a position to overhear them, then settled back in his chair. "Suppose we start with what this is really all about. You know that I'm sterile, so what is it you want?"

"I don't know you're sterile," she said solemnly. "I never did."

His long fingers curled into his palm until his hand had formed a fist; it was the only outward sign that his calm had altered. "What kind of game do you think you're playing, Sharon? A lot of years have passed since we've seen each other, but I don't believe for a minute that you've forgotten about the severe case of mumps I had when I was twelve that left me sterile."

"How could I forget—" The waiter's appearance cut off Sharon's retort, and she was forced to bide her time while he served them their drinks. Surreptitiously she studied Conall. In his dark blue suit, with ebony cuff links gleaming elegantly in the French cuffs of his white linen shirt, he looked formidable and powerfully masculine, completely sure of himself and his position in the world. There were times when she thought she must be out of her mind to go up against him, and this was one of those times. But the throbbingly empty feeling deep within her pushed her on.

When the waiter had once more departed, she spoke again. "How could I forget something that had such a great impact on my life? It was because of that case of mumps that you and your parents felt you should be tested to find out whether or not I was telling the truth. Do you know what your doubts did to me?"

"I know what they did to me."

"*You.* That was all that mattered, wasn't it? No one gave a thought to the young girl who had no social standing or money and who foolishly was claiming she was pregnant with your baby. Never mind that you'd been having sex with her for four months. With a great fortune and family tradition at stake, I'm sure your parents were extremely eager that the test results be the *correct* results."

"Are you suggesting my parents bribed someone to alter the results?" he asked, his voice suddenly ominous and quiet.

"I'm suggesting they might have felt they had a reason to lie. Or, for that matter, you might have."

"You're wrong, Sharon."

She sighed. There was no point in arguing with him, at least on this particular point, at least not now. "Okay, I'll rephrase what I was about to say. The doctor told you it was highly improbable that you could father a child because of an extremely low sperm count. But I am in a unique position to know better—because, Conall, ten years ago I became pregnant with your child. Your child, Conall, not Mark Bretton's, as he claimed. *Yours.*"

He opened his mouth, but something in the

center of his gut was hurting, preventing him from speaking. Lord help him. It had taken such a long time to get over her and what she had done to him. Now, after all these years, she had appeared, dredging up something he had worked hard to make peace with. And apparently he hadn't done as good a job as he had thought. Just saying the word *sterile* had left a bitter taste in his mouth. He took a deep drink of Scotch and waited a moment until his emotions were once more controlled.

"As I see it, I have two options," he said slowly. "The first is to consider that you are lying to me for some reason I have yet to discover. If this is the case, I need to find out what your reasons are and put a halt to anything that might hurt me or my family."

"Hurt the mighty Deverells? Who would dare to try?"

"You threatened."

"Did I?"

He exhaled heavily. "My second option is to consider that you are telling the truth. Now, if you are, which, by the way, is currently beyond my mental grasp, then I again have to consider the reasons why. Ten years have passed. You lost your baby. What is the point in rehashing it?"

"How very businesslike, Conall, outlining your options like that. It makes everything so plain, and it's such a chief-executive-officer thing to do. I'm truly impressed." She suddenly leaned forward, and her eyes sparked with anger. "I'm not, however, impressed with the fact that you haven't changed in all this time. You still refuse to see what is most obvious, most simple."

One black brow rose. "You're right. I left out a third option, the one that says you're crazy."

"I'm not crazy, Conall. All I want is a baby. It's a perfectly normal need for a woman."

"But you don't want just any baby. You want *my* baby."

She held up her hands and mimed applause. "That's exactly right. Congratulations. I think you've finally got it."

"What is this, Sharon? Revenge?"

"Revenge? Don't flatter yourself. I haven't been pining for you all these years. No, this whole idea came to me *after* I inherited Jake's note."

"Then if it's not revenge . . ."

"Vindication." She punched the tabletop with a finger for emphasis. "I want to prove to you that you were wrong to insist that the baby I was carrying, then lost, wasn't yours. Once that happens, I'll get out of your life again, this time of my own free will, this time forever."

He stared at her, trying to analyze, comprehend, understand. Tonight her hair fell straight around her face and onto her shoulders. In the subdued light of the restaurant, a faint hint of gold seemed to gleam beneath the ivory hue of her skin. The natural loveliness she had possessed as a young girl was still there, but it had matured, become more striking, more seductive. One thing hadn't changed, though. She had lied to him as a young girl, and she was lying to him now. She had to want money; it was the only thing that came close to making sense to him.

With a curse he pushed back from the table and stood. "Let's get out of here." After throwing several bills beside his barely touched Scotch, he reached for her arm and pulled her from the chair. "We've changed our mind," he told the startled waiter as they walked quickly past him. "We won't be having dinner after all."

Two

"This is not what I expected," Conall said, glancing around Sharon's apartment that was located on the top floor of an old brownstone.

Sharon followed his gaze, trying to see what it was that he found so unusual, but everything seemed ordinary to her. Though inexpensive, her furniture was comfortable and well maintained. She had invested in a good stereo system and a color television set. On one wall she had hung a blue and mauve quilt her grandmother had worked and given to her when she had been a young girl. Good prints, along with an occasional oil she had picked up from a sidewalk artist, covered the other walls. A basket she kept beside the sofa held her needlework. Mauve yarn spilled over its rim and down its sides, giving an untidy appearance. She should have put the basket away, she thought, but she hadn't known he would insist on coming back to the apartment with her.

Her first instinct had been to keep where she lived a secret from him. This apartment was the one place in the universe where she could come to be soothed when she was tense, comforted when she hurt, rest when she was tired. It was her retreat. In the end, though, since he still hadn't agreed to what she wanted, she had given in and let him know where she lived.

But it was just as she had feared. Standing in the middle of her small living room, he exuded waves of power that seemed as if they could threaten everything breakable in her home.

Luckily her heart was now inviolate to him.

She reached for the afghan she had crocheted one winter, the same afghan that had warmed her earlier that day, and hugged it to her.

He watched her, disturbed, feeling an absurd urge to try to pierce through to her center to see if she matched inside as well as out. "Frankly I expected your apartment to have a great deal less charm and personality."

A reluctant smile tugged at her lips. "I think there's a compliment in there somewhere, but it would take a great deal of ingenuity, not to mention energy to search for it."

Her smile drew his gaze. He supposed he had been too stunned to see her earlier at his office to notice the full, generous shape of her mouth before now. Then he remembered. He had once kissed that mouth until her lips were swollen. "I wouldn't have been surprised to find banks of calculators and computers," he said, "maybe even profit and loss charts on the walls and the television tuned to the Dow Jones averages."

She folded the afghan and returned it to the back of the couch. "You just described an office. Why would you think I lived in an office?"

"Maybe not an office, but something a bit more austere than this would have been in keeping with the all-business way you present yourself."

"You're the ultimate businessman. Are you trying to tell me your home isn't as comfortable as you and probably a team of decorators plus a slew of Deverell family possessions can make it?"

"You know what I mean."

She should have listened to her instincts, she told herself, and never have brought him here. He was trying to dissect her; she could almost feel the sharpness of his scalpel. "I have found over the years that appearance is very important when you're discussing business."

"Business? Was that what it was? I thought we were discussing me taking you to bed and making you pregnant."

She refused to let him unnerve her. "Actually, that's what *I've* been discussing. *You* have been avoiding giving me an answer. Would you like some coffee?"

"Yes. Black, please."

"It would never have crossed my mind to think that you took cream or sugar," she murmured, walking toward the door.

"Sharon?"

She stopped and looked back at him.

"What have you done to your hair?"

She frowned. "Nothing. Why?"

"It used to be curly."

Her face cleared. "Oh, it still is. I just blow-dry the curls out of it every morning. It's my experience that men don't take women in business seriously if they look like Shirley Temple."

"You *never* looked like Shirley Temple, and I can't remember ever withholding a promotion from one of my women executives because of her hairstyle."

"Then they're lucky. That is, if that's the truth."

She disappeared through a door, and in a moment he heard the sound of cabinet doors opening and closing. She didn't trust him at all, he thought, on *any* subject. But that was fine, because he didn't trust her either.

Across the room, a shelf held a dozen or more Hummel children. Closer inspection showed a figurine of a boy going off to school, a book satchel on his back, an eager expression on his face. Another figurine showed two children on a seesaw, another, a blond-haired little girl smelling a daisy.

He reached out a finger to touch the daisy, but quickly pulled it back when he sensed Sharon's presence. He turned to find her leaning against the doorjamb, watching him, her arms crossed beneath her breasts.

"The coffee's perking. It won't take long."

"You have quite a collection," he said, inclining his head toward the shelf.

"They make me happy."

He threw another glance at the assortment of stoneware children. "In what way?"

She felt a sharp twinge, the scalpel again. "I don't know. They just do." Perhaps it would be appropriate for her to try a little dissection herself. "Isn't there anything that simply makes you happy?"

It was a strange question, and one intended to put him on the spot. "Everything in my life makes me happy. I've arranged it that way."

She stared at him for a moment, listening to the echo of what he had just said reverberate in her mind. *I've arranged it that way.* It was a reminder of what the Deverell power was capable of. There was nothing they couldn't "arrange." If one of their daughters wanted to turn the family home into the most exclusive resort in America, it could be arranged. If one of their sons wanted to be a United States senator, and then, after a reasonable amount of time had passed, the president, it could be arranged. If another of their sons decided he didn't want to acknowledge parentage of a child, it could be arranged.

It was also a reminder of how carefully she would have to proceed if and when he agreed to honor Jake's promise. No, she corrected herself. Not *if*. It had to be *when*. "The coffee must be ready."

She returned to the kitchen, and Conall took a seat on the sofa. Directly across from him was a false fireplace. A porcelain English spaniel lounged on its hearth, a wreath of flowers woven together by a mauve ribbon hung above its mantel. A stained-glass hummingbird hovered at a window, suspended by a nearly invisible plastic filament.

His gaze moved restlessly around the room and stopped at a small bottle of perfume sitting on a table, obviously out of place. Had she been applying it to her skin as she'd walked through the room, then, perhaps running late for their dinner appointment, set it down and walked out the door to meet him?

He tugged at his tie, freeing the red silk from its knots so that it hung loose. They should have stayed in the damned restaurant, he thought. Her apartment bothered him. It was overwhelmingly feminine with a touch of the whimsical, and it reminded him too much of Sharon as a young girl—or, rather, what he had thought she was.

Undoing the top buttons of his shirt, he cast his mind back to the time he had been twenty-two, just finishing Harvard, and she had been a sweet, fresh, lovely eighteen, working in a men's clothing shop near the college. He had gone into the shop to buy a sweater and had walked out with a date with her.

From the first he had been wild about her, and she had seemed to reciprocate the feelings. Their relationship had quickly escalated to a sexual one with an almost mystical ease and naturalness.

They had known each other just a few weeks when his friend, Mark Bretton, had begun to whisper stories in his ear about Sharon. He had laughed off the stories, believing that Mark wanted Sharon for himself. But as the days passed, Mark continued telling him tales. Then one day, after he and Sharon had been seeing each other for a few months, she had come to him and told him she was pregnant. He remembered the hope and the hesitancy in her eyes, and most of all he remembered the fear. And that was when everything Mark had been telling him came rushing back.

He went to his parents. Visibly distressed, they reminded him that his bout with the mumps had been so severe, the possibility existed he was sterile.

His test results had confirmed their fears and his. He had left the doctor's office in a daze.

Back then, he had never looked far beyond the present. There was no reason to. Because of his name, because of the fortune he would inherit on his next birthday, his way was made in life. The future, he had thought, held only possibilities.

Accustomed as he was to this mindset, the knowledge of his sterility devastated him—almost as much as having to face the fact that Sharon had been unfaithful to him and was carrying another man's child.

He had gone back to her and told her he wasn't the father of her baby, that it was impossible. She had stared at him, completely without expression. Then she had turned and run out the door. Shortly afterward he heard she lost the baby.

Since that time, all thoughts of her had been relegated to an unlighted place in his mind beyond his conscious awareness. But his response to her after her sudden reappearance in his life clued him to the fact that his unconscious mind had kept her memory close.

He looked up as she carried in a tray with two steaming hot cups of coffee on it. She placed it on the table in front of the couch, then chose to sit on the corner opposite him.

While she poured the coffee, she cast surreptitious glances at him. He still wore the dark blue suit she had seen him in at his office earlier, but by unknotting his tie and unbuttoning his shirt, he had managed to add a strongly dangerous quality to his already powerful sexuality. She could cope, she told herself; her interest in him wasn't personal. She handed him a cup and picked up her own.

"I was sorry to hear that you lost the baby."

Her hand faltered, and coffee spilled onto her saucer. She blotted the liquid up with a napkin. "Then you knew. I wasn't sure since you never tried to see me again."

"How did you expect me to react, Sharon? It wasn't my baby."

She turned her head away, but right before she did he caught a glimpse of her expression. The hurt and bitterness he saw gave him pause. Had those feelings made it difficult for her to come to him today? Or had they made it easy for her?

She put a teaspoon of sugar into her coffee and stirred. "Have you made up your mind about what you're going to do?"

To give himself an extra moment before he answered, he took a sip of the steaming liquid, found it too hot, and set it on the table. "There's nothing to decide, Sharon. I cannot make you pregnant. It would be physically impossible."

She tried to bank down the anger that instantly flared. "You sound so sure of yourself. You're not even willing to acknowledge the possibility that I could be telling the truth about the baby being yours."

"If you're right, why didn't you argue with me back then? Why did you run out into the night like you did?"

"I was incredibly hurt that you didn't believe me when I first told you. I thought we loved each other, and I knew I'd done nothing to deserve your suspicion. Then waiting for the results of the test shredded my nerves. The final denial from you just about destroyed me."

"Destroyed *you*? Lord, Sharon, you were the first girl I'd ever loved. What do you think the knowledge that you had been unfaithful did to me?"

"Frankly, I don't care, because, you see, I know what I suffered when you turned your back on me."

He rubbed his eyes with a thumb and finger, and then raised his head and looked at her. "Don't you understand I would love for you to be right? The fact that I'm sterile has affected my whole life."

Just for an instant something opened in him, and she caught a glimpse of private torment. Surprisingly, she felt a pang of sympathy; she promptly squelched it. This man didn't need anyone's sympathy. He was a Deverell. He had only to lift a finger and whatever he desired came to him. "You keep using the word *sterile*. But as I recall, what the doctor said was that you had a low sperm count. There's a big difference between those two things."

His jaw tightened. "In this case, semantics don't change the meaning. The percentage chance he estimated for me was and is negligible."

The sign of his stubbornness strengthened her

determination. She put aside her cup and clasped her hands together. "Haven't you ever once considered that you could have been wrong?"

"No."

"No," she repeated, indignation rising. "A Deverell decree. It is said, it will be." She sat forward. "All right, Conall, just for the sake of argument, let's say you are absolutely right. You are physically incapable of fathering a child. Then tell me, what do you have to lose by doing what you have to do for two weeks to make me pregnant? It's my understanding that most men enjoy it."

His head snapped around. "*Men* enjoy it? Are you saying you don't think women do? Or you? What about you?"

She shrugged, extremely uncomfortable with the sudden turn of the conversation, and she had no one to blame but herself for not watching her words more carefully. "It doesn't matter about me."

She didn't want to admit to him that his lovemaking had given her great happiness and pleasure. It was a matter of pride, plus she was aware of the possibility that he might in some way use the knowledge as a weapon against her.

"Sharon, you can't tell me I didn't satisfy you. There were too many times when—" He bit off his words and shook his head, disgusted with himself for remembering.

She nearly groaned aloud. She didn't want to think about sex with Conall. This time she tried to select her words more cautiously, and at the same time she inadvertently ended up telling him at least part of the truth. "Look, don't let your ego get in the way here. I enjoyed the act because at the time I loved you, or, rather, I thought I loved you. When we were together it was emotionally satisfying. That was all that was important to me."

He stared at her. "The *act*?"

"Conall, I didn't know any better. If you'll remember, you were my first lover. I was very young, and, as a matter of fact, so were you. But none of this is important. We need to get back to the subject at hand."

She was right, it wasn't important. But his memories of that time were about how immensely she had satisfied him. "What was the subject?"

"I asked you what you have to lose by being with me for two weeks."

"Being with you," he repeated. "I don't believe I've ever heard as many euphemisms in the space of such a short time. You have the oddest way of putting things, but I assume you mean 'being with me' in a sexual sense."

A hint of color slowly climbed her neck. She nodded. "You know I do."

The blushing was a habit he remembered from long ago. He had always found the trait intriguing, but now he had other things on his mind. Emotions and memories of the past and present were colliding, making him feel as if he were standing in the middle of a battlefield. Except the battle was taking place inside of him. Shots were being fired. Blows were being landed. And they hurt.

He sighed. "I don't know what I have to lose, Sharon, but I'm sure if I think long enough, I'll come up with something. You see, I have no reason to trust you."

Her backbone stiffened. "And I have even less reason to trust you, but I suggest we overcome our mutual distrust. I'm not asking much."

"That's a matter of opinion. As you have somehow managed to observe—how did you put it?—

I don't engage in indiscriminate sexual affairs." He was half angry with her, wholly frustrated, and most definitely suspicious. But *no one* could have gotten him to leave, not just yet, at any rate. "What about artificial insemination? For what you want, it would be much more cut and dried, much less messy. And best of all, you wouldn't have to try to force a man into your bed who doesn't want to be there."

Her lips firmed. "I told you in your office today, artificial insemination wouldn't suit my purposes. Aside from the reason I've already stated, when my child asks where he comes from, I don't want to have to say a syringe. I also don't want to leave the choice of my child's father to a lab technician."

"You'd get to choose physical traits, background, things such as that, wouldn't you?"

"I'd know the color of the donor's hair and eyes, but it's not the same as knowing the man. I assume that by the end of two weeks, I'll know at least some of your likes and dislikes."

"At least in bed you will."

He'd deliberately made a suggestive remark and was rewarded when color rushed up her neck again. What kind of modern-day woman flushed at the idea of being in bed with a man, especially when it was her idea in the first place?

"Within reason," she was saying, "I'll be able to satisfy my child's curiosity without once mentioning labs, test tubes, or syringes."

"Since you seem set on trying to prove I can father a child, what if I agreed to supply the sperm to the laboratory?"

"That's not good enough," she said with a definite shake of her head. "Even if I got pregnant, you could say that the lab had made a mistake, switched vials, something, *anything* to keep from acknowledging the truth to yourself."

"The truth being that I am capable of fathering a child and did so all those years ago."

"That's right."

Let the subject drop, he told himself. "I have to say you've thought of almost everything."

Her chin went up a notch, the way it had in his office. This time he read a vulnerability into the defensive gesture.

"Not almost. I've thought of *everything*."

Get up and leave, he told himself. "No, I'm afraid there's one thing you haven't thought of."

"What?"

Why in the hell wasn't he taking his own advice? From the cradle, young girls and then women had tried to get him, his name, and his money, in that order. Many times he had walked away from far less explosive situations than this one. Why didn't he now? He spread his arm along the back of the couch until his hand was within touching distance of her. "What if we're not sexually compatible?"

"Sex— What do you mean?"

He shrugged. "What if there's no passion between us?"

Her pulse picked up a beat and she frowned. "There doesn't have to be passion. This is a business deal, pure and simple."

The funny thing was, he really believed she meant it. "You may look at it as a business deal, Sharon, but I'm not some circus animal who can perform on command. No." He shook his head. "You want me to perform in bed, you're going to have to make me feel passion."

Once more color flooded her face.

He studied the color for a moment, then said quietly, "Come here."

"What?"

"Come here." He took her arm and pulled her across the couch to him. When she was close enough, he cupped the side of her face with his hand.

She swallowed convulsively. "What are you doing?"

"Nothing yet. But in a minute I'm going to kiss you." His eyes glittered as he gazed at her lips and stroked his thumb up and down her cheek. "You don't have any objections, do you?"

Her heart was pounding loudly; her nerves were jumping out of control. Her tongue moistened her bottom lip. "As a matter of fact, I do."

His thumb smoothed across her lip, wiping up the moistness laid down by her tongue. "Why?"

"It—it's just not necessary, that's all."

"Okay," he said. "I guess I could skip the kiss."

Relief flooded through her. "Good."

"And I could go right to caressing your breasts."

Her eyes widened in alarm.

He slowly withdrew his hand from her face, sat back in the corner of the couch, and eyed her thoughtfully. "I don't know what you expected, Sharon, but I'm not going to spend two minutes having sex with a woman who doesn't excite me, much less two weeks. I think we'd better forget the whole thing." He crooked his arm, shot back a white cuff, and glanced at his watch. "It's late. I must leave."

"No, wait! Don't leave."

One black brow arched in inquiry, in demand.

"All right, we can kiss."

He was silent for a moment. "You sound like you'd rather I pull your fingernails out one by one. Ten years may have passed, Sharon, but I don't remember you being this reticent."

"I wasn't. I'm not." She waved a helpless hand. "This is just all very awkward."

"Trying to force someone to do something he doesn't want to do always is. Surely you took that into account."

"You really are a bastard, aren't you?"

His face softened with a slow smile. "That's not the way to do it, Sharon. You've got to make me want you." His voice dropped to a sexy, cajoling whisper. "Come on. Try."

She hesitated.

"You may have your schedule worked out, but I would have to do a hell of a lot of juggling before I could break away from my work for any length of time. You've got to make it worth my while."

"You—"

"Ah-ah. Unless you're about to utter an endearment, I'd keep quiet if I were you." His eyes narrowed on her stormy expression. "Make my blood boil, Sharon. Then you can call me anything you like."

It was too much of a temptation to resist, she decided, already running choice names through her mind, completely forgetting her ultimate objective. She leaned forward and pressed her lips hard against his for what she considered an overly long time.

He didn't move.

She pulled away and looked at him.

"Try again," he suggested softly.

This time she parted her lips and brushed them back and forth against his. He didn't stir, and when she pulled away, she saw challenge in his eyes.

"Well, you could help," she burst out.

"This was your idea," he reminded her.

Yes, it was, she thought, and right at this moment she was thinking it was a very bad idea.

She had known she would have to be held in his arms, that he would more than likely kiss her and caress her, and that eventually she would have to go to bed with him. She hadn't liked the idea, but she understood it had to be done and she looked on it as the price she had to pay to get what she wanted.

Unfortunately and for some odd reason, she hadn't really considered the reality. *This* was the reality: the way the combined musk and spice scent of his body had entered her brain and was clouding her thinking, the way heat had begun to congest her lungs.

She couldn't go through with it.

Dammit! She had to go through with it!

She wanted, overwhelmingly needed, a baby. A child. Someone to nurture and take care of, someone to watch over and help grow into adulthood. Someone to whom she could give all her love.

She had to continue. If she made him feel the things he said were necessary for him to feel, then he would agree to do what she wanted, and she would get her baby. It was as simple as that.

"Sharon?"

She leaned forward again, and this time she put her arms around his neck and kissed him with urgency, with open lips and thrusting tongue, with passion that was acted.

He saw straight through her feigned eagerness. Still, her pretense gave him a hint of what it might be like if she weren't playacting, and it made him curious. He settled farther back into the corner of the couch and took her with him. "Easy, easy," he murmured against her lips. "Let's go a little slower and see if we can't make a real fire."

Her sudden stiffness didn't deter him. He lightly fastened his teeth on her lower lip, and taking his time, he nipped and licked at the sweet, soft flesh. Surprisingly, the more he tasted of her, the hungrier he became. But he forced himself to remain patient until, almost imperceptibly, he felt her begin to relax, her body softening by degrees as little by little she seemed to melt against him, and her contours melded more perfectly to his. Then he slipped his tongue between her parted lips and began a mating dance with her tongue.

Her heart gave a kick against his chest, then begin to race, and his own heart responded the same way. It was crazy, he thought, coming alive with her like this after all these years. He had started this kiss out of curiosity to see how she would react. Not once had he considered how *he* would react. He had approached the kiss as one might idly sample a smorgasbord, to see if there was anything he liked.

He liked everything. Having her against him, her open mouth working beguilingly and persuasively on his, had him aroused beyond belief. He tightened his hold on her and took her breast into his hand.

Sharon couldn't breathe for the wanting that had taken her unawares, and now she was suffocating in the heat being generated by his kisses. She didn't want to respond to him. She needed to stop him, but for the moment it was beyond her ability to do so. She was desperate for his damnably sweet, fiery kisses.

His hand smoothed back and forth across the soft wool that covered her breasts, her full shape exciting him. Soon he felt her nipple stiffen, and intense pleasure surged through him at the proof that passion was growing in her as it was in him.

He slid down against the couch's cushioned pillows so that he was half lying and she was over him. His blood had heated, thickened, a fever had taken over his brain. He grasped a handful of her skirt and drew it upward until it was around her waist. Then he delved beneath the lace edge of her panties to her firm, round bottom.

She heard herself moan just as panic began to edge into her consciousness. She tried to push against him, but she was barely able to move.

His arousal pressed against her, his long fingers kneaded her flesh, creating a magically wild, sensuous feeling. It was only a matter of time, she knew, before he would be caressing her in another, more intimate place. She was already moist from anticipation, but she couldn't allow it to happen. If she didn't call a halt to this soon, she would embarrass herself, like someone starved losing control at a banquet.

"Conall," she said breathlessly. "Stop."

He made an indistinguishable sound and arched his hips up to her. Through the silk of her panties she felt the pressure and fire shoot through her. Reality was slipping away, and she reached out for a lifeline. "Conall . . ."

This time he heard the tinge of alarm in her voice, but a compelling need was driving him. She was so soft, her curves so enticing, her taste so sweet.

"Conall."

The next moment she was free and on her feet. Her chest heaved as she tried to draw a deep breath, her limbs trembled, her skin was flushed. "I'm sorry. We can't do this."

Slowly, with effort, he sat up and straightened his clothes. "Why not?" he asked, his words clipped, his tone harsh. "I thought it was what you wanted."

"No." Her fingers entwined and held hard. "What I want is for you to make me pregnant."

He let out a string of curses that charged the

air between them. "*If* such a thing were possible, and *if* we had continued as we were going, that might have happened."

"Not *now*! *Now* is the wrong time! If you had looked at the chart I gave you, you would have seen that."

Conall jerked to his feet. "I don't understand what's going on here, and I don't think you do either. Out of the blue today you show up at my office with a seventy-year-old note that's not worth the paper it's written on, and a totally outrageous, not to mention impossible, proposition. Documents and charts aside, I don't think you've thought this whole thing through."

"You're wrong," she said, drawing another deep breath. "I've thought through everything very carefully. This situation is and will continue to be uncomfortable, awkward, and unorthodox, to say the very least. But I'm willing to suffer through it, and you're going to have to make up your mind to suffer through it too."

"Suffer? Is that what we were just doing?"

"Bastard."

"You've already called me that. Think of something new, Sharon."

"Damn you, you've *got* to honor your grandfather's promise."

"I don't see it that way."

"Then change your point of view. I went through hell because you declared yourself infertile. You owe me, Conall, and what I want is a baby."

Three

Conall tapped the report on his desk and smiled at the tall, sandy-haired man across from him. "Excellent job, as always."

Amarillo Smith gave a brief nod. "Glad to have been of help."

"As usual, your work is top-notch. This report tells me everything I need to know, both positive and negative, on Dugan Industries, and it gives me an insight into the personality of Jules Dugan. The information will be invaluable."

The two creases in Amarillo's cheeks that normally showed as vertical lines deepened. "That's our intention."

While Amarillo laid a booted foot over the opposite knee, Conall studied him. He had known the man for about three years, since before Nico DiFrenza's marriage to his cousin, Caitlin. Shortly after the marriage, Nico and Amarillo left the Boston police department and opened an investigative and security firm serving big business. Whether a company wanted information on another company for help on a proposed takeover, an upcoming lawsuit, or in uncovering leaks,

Amarillo and Nico were the best. Conall used their services frequently.

He considered Amarillo a friend, even though he knew he might have to wait a long time before he learned everything there was to know about him. But there was no doubt in his mind that he could trust him with the most sensitive and secretive information.

"I've checked on Caitlin and the baby, so I know they're doing fine. How's Nico?"

The creases deepened even further as a wry grin split Amarillo's face. "I'm having a hard time getting him into the office these days, and when he does make it in, he stays only a few hours. He seems to think there's never been a baby boy like little Deverell Niccolo DiFrenza. He also seems to be under the impression that he is single-handedly inventing fatherhood."

A week ago, Conall would have laughed. But Sharon's reappearance in his life had reminded him that he would never be able to father a child. He was extremely happy for Nico and Caitlin, but he envied Nico his pride in his new son.

He pushed away from his desk and stood. "I've got a problem, Rill."

"What can I do to help?"

It was typical of Amarillo to cut straight to the bottom line. The problem was Conall didn't have the faintest idea what Rill could do to help. He didn't even know why he felt the urge to bring him in on what was happening, except Amarillo had one of the coolest heads in a crisis situation he had ever encountered. As succinctly as possible he told him the entire story. He finished with, "Hell, Rill, she wants me for stud service."

Powerful shoulders shrugged beneath a western-cut suede jacket. "She wants to use you, so you use her instead."

Conall shook his head. "It's not that easy."

"Keeping a lovely woman in bed for two weeks would be some men's dream."

"Yeah, well, not mine." He said it, then immediately knew it wasn't true if the lovely woman was Sharon.

"Okay, so I'll put her under my microscope. By the time I'm through, I'll know what color polish she puts on her toenails and how many rollers it takes to set her hair."

He hesitated. "I'd rather hold off on that."

Amarillo eyed Conall thoughtfully. "You know, Conall, there might be a relatively easy way to find out if she's lying or not. Be tested again."

He shook his head. "No." He couldn't bring himself to go through the humiliation of the procedure and the ultimate pain it would cause when the doctor gave him the same results he had the last time.

"Then tell her to get lost and to hell with her."

"No."

Amarillo exhaled heavily. "Conall, I've just presented you with every alternative I can think of."

"I know, but none of them is acceptable to me." He grimaced. "I've tried to break this down into one, two, three. A, B, C. But it's not that simple. What happened in our past keeps getting in my way."

"Then the best advice I can give you is get into the present. That and let me investigate her."

"Investigation is out," he murmured, then focused on what Amarillo had said about the present. He felt helpless without a course of action, but Amarillo was right. To formulate a course of action, he needed to deal from the present, decide what he wanted in the here and now.

Looked at from that perspective, it was simple. He wanted Sharon.

*   *   *

Sharon opened her front door, then stepped back. Conall entered, vital and electric in a black evening suit. When he had called earlier and said he had made up his mind and would be over, she hadn't been able to guess what his decision might be. She still couldn't. His expression was unreadable. She hoped her expression was equally enigmatic.

Somehow, though, she didn't have much confidence in her ability to hide her nerves. It had been approximately forty-eight hours since she had last seen him. During that time she had dredged up every possible mistake she felt she had made with him in their two recent encounters. And she had put herself through torture wondering what he was thinking.

Now everything she had done in the past ten months had come down to this moment. If he said no, her whole life would be drastically changed. She would have to reformulate her goals, make new plans. But most of all, she would be left to contend with the incredible, awful void in her life that had finally driven her to go to him in the first place.

The idea of having Conall make her pregnant had only firmed in her mind ten months before. But in ways she was sure she hadn't even thought of yet, Conall had shaped her life. If it all deadended here, she didn't know what would be left.

She noticed him casting a disapproving gaze around her apartment and had no idea why. But as before, his presence seemed to threaten all things fragile, and she was reminded he was a man who commanded an empire. He had no need to be careful or subtle. "Would you like to sit down?"

He turned to her with an abruptness that took her off guard. "Why do you live in such a small place?"

"Excuse me?"

"You must make a good salary."

"I do." Wariness laced her tone. "You saw my tax statements."

"I didn't look at them. There was no need, since I knew there wouldn't be a baby involved."

She almost staggered as despair hit her like a physical blow. "Then your answer is no."

"I didn't say that. I said I knew there wouldn't be a baby involved, and there won't be, because I'm sterile. But I've decided to spend the two weeks with you."

"I don't understand," she said slowly.

He smiled and propped his elbow on the fireplace mantel. "Our affair was hot despite the fact that you were also sleeping with Mark Bretton."

"I did no such thing, Conall."

He found himself wishing like hell he could believe her, but he went on as if she hadn't spoken. "We definitely had something back then, you and I. It was sweet and wild and uninhibited. Under normal circumstances it would most likely have run its course and fizzled out as most youthful affairs do. But ours didn't have a chance to end naturally. It hit a solid wall of lies and infidelity—"

"They weren't *my* lies."

He managed a shrug. "Whatever, it ended suddenly and unexpectedly, and we were both, for different reasons, left with bitterness, plus I imagine a host of other unresolved feelings. I'd like to tell you that I haven't thought of you over the years, but I'm not sure that's true. And now, for your own reasons, you have chosen to come back into my life."

He was making it sound as if she had invaded his life, and she felt compelled to point out, "For a very brief period of time."

"Okay, brief. But whatever the length of time, I don't think highly of your reasons for showing up again."

"Then why are you agreeing?"

"Because two days ago, on that couch over there, I learned you can still make me want you." He nodded at the color that immediately climbed upward under her skin. "That's still the same too. We may find other things that are also the same. But one thing I will not have repeated, Sharon, are the lies."

"I never lied to you, Conall. The baby was yours."

The expression in his eyes turned frost cold, and his whole demeanor hardened, darkened. "All right. You've said it. I heard. Now, you—don't—have—to—say—it—again."

An icy shudder skimmed through her. "You don't want to spend this time with me."

"Would you like me to show you how wrong you are? Over there on the couch? Or perhaps in your bedroom?"

She shook her head, hating the helpless way he made her feel.

"I've made up my mind, Sharon. You want to use me to make you pregnant, no matter how often I've told you that it is impossible. So fine. You can use me as long as I can use you."

She had an inexplicable urge to run, and she had to remind herself that she was in her own apartment, a place she had always felt safe. Why wasn't it working now? "I don't know what you mean," she said slowly.

"I'm being as up front with you as I know how,

Sharon. You're obviously still in my system. I figure two weeks should just about get you out."

A look of real distress crossed her face. "No. This won't work. Not at all."

His head tilted to an arrogant angle. "Why not? I'm agreeing to what you want."

"Yes, but you're making it all too *personal*."

His laugh was brusque. "You mean because I've dared to hint that I'm going to enjoy the hell out of the time we'll be together? Sharon, that's what it's all about."

"But I never intended for us to become involved again. I wanted only to get—"

"Pregnant, I know." He pushed away from the mantel and came to stand by her. "You ruled out artificial insemination. Sorry, but that leaves only one other method that I know of. And there's no way a man and a woman can get any more personal and involved than by having sex." He touched a baby-fine curl by her cheek that had escaped from the severity of her otherwise straight hairstyle. "Don't you remember?"

There was an unbearable pressure in her chest. Breathing was suddenly difficult. She was a fool, she told herself. A stupid, stupid fool. She shouldn't be panicking like this. It was just that when she had thought of them performing the sex act, it had always been with an emotionally formal distance between them.

Still, she assured herself, everything would be all right. Her goal was to have a baby, and she couldn't let herself be thrown off track just because he intended to have . . . fun. She could handle it. She had to. Having a child was the most important thing in the world to her. And vindicating herself was the next most important.

"Will you sign the document I had drawn up?" she asked.

"I will have the medical test for sexual disease, but I will not sign anything else."

She wavered, then remembered—the document had been to ease *his* mind, not hers. She lifted her head and met his gaze. "All right, it's a deal."

He smiled, and disconcertingly she thought she noticed a slight softening in him.

"Very good," he said, the baby-fine curl drawing another flicking touch from his fingers. "Now, go get dressed. Something a bit more formal than your jeans."

"What?"

He waved a vague hand. "There's a charity function. Normally I wouldn't bother, but it's a chance for us to catch my cousin Caitlin out of the nursery."

"What?" she said again, realizing she didn't only sound stupid, she felt stupid.

"My cousin, Caitlin. She'll be there, along with her husband, Nico, and we can ask about the availability of one of the family suites at SwanSea."

"Why would we want to do that?"

"Because that's where we're going for the next two weeks. By the way, just exactly *when* are we going?" He gave her a grin that from anyone else she would have interpreted as engaging. "I didn't read your chart."

"My fertile period should start in approximately five days."

"Five days. That should give me enough time to get things settled at the office."

She stared at him, feeling as though a windstorm had caught her up in its force and was hurling her toward an unknown destination.

"Why SwanSea? I mean, why do we need to go out of town?"

"Because if I stay in Boston, my office will feel I'm still accessible. On the other hand, they view

SwanSea as sacrosanct and don't bother me there. Besides, it's one of my favorite places in the world."

Maybe it *was* a good idea, she thought. Perhaps she would be better able to relax in a place that to her was totally impersonal, without memories.

"Unless you'd like to stay here and get a head start on the fun and games, I suggest you go change."

The urge to take the course of least resistance and do as he said was strong, but the urge to reassert herself was even stronger. "What I would like is to stay here and have you leave. You don't need me to be with you when you ask your cousin, and I can't see a reason in the world why I should have to go to this function with you."

"No?" With a few steps he closed the distance between them.

Automatically she took a step backward.

"That's the reason," he said softly. "You get nervous if I even come near you. How do you suppose you'll react when you're in bed with me?"

She crossed her arms beneath her breasts. "I'll be fine."

"Will you?" He reached out and skimmed his fingertips down one silky cheek.

She jerked away.

He slipped his hands into his trouser pockets. "You obviously don't feel comfortable with me, and knowing that, I sure as hell won't be comfortable with you. Being in bed with you would be like being in bed with a bundle of thorns. The first time I tried to take you into my arms, I'd get stuck."

"No—"

"I don't like to bleed, Sharon."

And she didn't either, she thought, which was part of her problem. Aversion didn't make her shy

away from him. Fear did. She was terrified that
her own responses would betray her in some way,
and give him power to hurt her.

"All I'm suggesting is that we spend a little time
together and blunt the sharpest edges."

"I'm not sure spending one evening together is
going to accomplish much."

"It will be a beginning."

She sighed. Much as she hated to admit it, he
was again right. She had to overcome the ten-
dency to react to him like a frightened virgin. Perhaps a social situation in which they would be
together but not alone would help matters.

"All right," she said, turning and heading for
the bedroom. "Make yourself comfortable. It won't
take me long to change."

As she had climbed her firm's ladder to the top,
she had been required to attend evening functions, so she had an extensive wardrobe of suit-
able dresses. She chose a gold one made of a wool,
silk, and cashmere blend that fell in soft, fluid
folds to her feet. It had long sleeves, a high round
neck, and a deep cowl back. She donned the
dress, then in a minimum amount of time, pulled
her hair off her neck and twisted and pinned the
long strands into a chignon. After putting on
dangling gold and bronze earrings, she applied a
light makeup to eyes, cheeks, and mouth, trans-
ferred necessities into an evening purse and
walked back into the living room.

Conall threw down a magazine he had been
reading and stood. His dark-eyed gaze swept over
her. "You look lovely," he said, his voice husky.
"Really lovely. Shall we go?"

"Of course you can have one of the suites,"
Caitlin said with a toss of her cinnamon-colored

hair. "Why are you even asking? You know the fourth floor is always set aside for the family's exclusive use."

Conall shrugged. "I thought I should at least notify you."

Her green-gold eyes sparkled with amusement. "There's something else going on here, isn't there? You hardly ever come to these charity functions anymore. Why did you come tonight? Does this have something to do with your date for the evening?"

A reluctant smile tugged at his mouth. "Try not to let your imagination get the better of you, Caitlin. It's a very unattractive trait."

"Would you like me to hit you?" she asked sweetly.

"No. Just notify your manager that I'll be bringing a guest."

"Who?"

"None of your business."

"Okay, I'll accept that. Basically, because as soon as you arrive, I'll be able to find out who's with you. By the way, you'll have the fourth floor all to yourself. Nico and I don't plan to go up for a while, and your parents just came back. Mother and Quinn have become quite the homebodies since their marriage and their move to their new place in the country. Uncle Seldon and his advisers held a political powwow up there a few weeks ago, but now he's back out on the road." She grinned. "I must say, I'm delighted you'll be staying so long. I can't remember the last time you've taken more than a three-day weekend."

"Then I guess it was about time." His smile grew until it was full blown. "So how is Wonder Baby?"

Caitlin laughed. "Dev is totally brilliant. We're thinking of enrolling him in Harvard soon. And by the way, his nursery is beginning to resemble a toy store. Every day new packages arrive from his uncle Conall."

"I want him to have a choice of things to do. Some variety. Poor kid, I'm sure he's bored. I mean, all he does day in and day out is sleep, eat, and look at you and Nico make fools of yourselves over him."

"Very funny. Now tell me about Sharon."

Conall threw a glance over his shoulder. Across the table, Nico and Sharon were engaged in conversation. As he watched, she smiled at Nico. The smile was a trifle shy, but unlike the stilted, hard-edged smiles she had been giving him, it was genuine. Unsettled, he turned back to Caitlin. "Do you like her?"

Caitlin checked the emerald-studded watch on her wrist. "You only introduced us an hour ago, but from what I can tell, she seems very nice. The question is, do you like her? And will she be going with you to SwanSea?"

He shifted restlessly. "So Dev's going to be a Harvard man? Don't you think you should at least wait until he's potty trained?"

Caitlin sat forward. "How *really* interesting. You're evading the subject."

"Just shut up and play along."

Caitlin's laughter pealed out, bright and happy. "All right, all right. Well, let's see. The other day, Dev distinctly said *mama*."

Conall looked properly amazed. "No!"

She nodded. "It's true. Nico is sure he said *dada*, but I know for a fact he said *mama*."

Sharon surreptitiously gazed at the cousins, one so beautiful, the other so handsome. They sat close together, talking animatedly yet low, making it impossible for her to hear their conversation. But it was fascinating to watch them together. The two Deverell cousins were marked with the same qualities of ease, assurance, and a sense of belonging. She couldn't imagine they had ever had a doubt in their life. She envied them.

"The Deverells have a unique quality all their own, don't they?" Nico asked, obviously noticing where her attention was directed. "It's as if the substance of their bone marrow is different from the normal person's. They have an unspoken, unquestioning belief in themselves and the manageability of the world around them."

Her baby would be one of those self-assured Deverells. The thought hit Sharon with a jolt. Funny she hadn't viewed it that way before. But there was nothing she wanted more than to instill in her child a certainty and faith in himself and his own powers, and if his being a Deverell would make her job any easier, so be it.

She turned to Nico, a man who had an abundance of the same traits. "I understand you're also a Deverell."

"I can't deny it," he said with a smile, "But my sister and I were raised DiFrenzas, and that's how we think of ourselves."

Her gaze darted to the dance floor, where his sister, Angelica, with her long dark hair streaming down her back, gracefully glided to the music with her date. "Your sister is extremely beautiful."

"Thank you. I think so."

Her gaze continued over the dance floor to the tall, sandy-haired man named Amarillo Smith. He and his date, a sophisticated-looking blonde, also had places at their table. At the moment the blonde was doing her best to enchant him, with her body pressed closely to his, her head thrown back, her eyes gazing up into his, her lips parted.

Somehow Sharon didn't think her tactics were working.

"Would you like to dance?" Conall asked.

Startled, she looked up at him. She hadn't seen him leave Caitlin and walk around the table. "I—"

He grasped her elbow and helped her to her feet. "Nico, you don't mind if I steal her from you, do you?"

Nico grinned. "Actually, I do. If you take her away, I'll be forced to ask my wife to dance."

Much to Sharon's surprise, Caitlin, society's princess, picked up a bread roll and threw it at her husband. "You'll pay for that, Nico DiFrenza."

"I can't wait," he murmured, a glitter in his dark eyes.

"*Conall*, how nice to see you!"

Sharon felt Conall start. She turned to see an older couple, their faces wreathed with smiles. She immediately recognized them as Conall's parents and went ice cold.

"We didn't know you would be here," his mother said, an elegant woman with silver hair and an array of large, perfect diamonds sparkling at her neck, her ears, and on her fingers. "Why didn't you call? We could have made arrangements to have you at our table."

"It was a last-minute decision," Conall said, leaning down to kiss his mother's cheek. "And Caitlin said there would be room at her table."

"Hello, Aunt Rebecca, Uncle Lucas," Caitlin called from her position across the table.

Rebecca Deverell sent Caitlin a warm smile. "Hello, darling." She reached around her son and patted Nico on the shoulder. "You're looking much better than you were when Dev was born. You were so pale that night, we were very concerned."

Nico grinned sheepishly.

Sharon had been standing, paralyzed under Lucas Deverell's acute scrutiny, and now she felt the force of his wife's attention. "Introduce us to your date, Conall."

"I'll be glad to," he said smoothly. "Mother, this is Sharon Graham. Sharon, this is my mother and father, Rebecca and Lucas Deverell."

The lights of the room seemed to dim. She felt herself sway, then Conall's hand was against her back, supporting her. "How do you do," she murmured.

Lucas Deverell nodded pleasantly enough, but there was a sharpness in his eyes that made her stomach churn sickeningly.

"Sharon Graham," Rebecca repeated thoughtfully. "That name sounds so familiar. Have we—?"

"No," Conall said, abruptly interrupting his mother, "you've never met. Now, if you'll excuse us, we were just about to dance."

"Of course, darling. But do come by our table later, won't you?"

"If it's possible."

Conall guided her out onto the dance floor and drew her into his arms.

She barely felt his left hand as it slid around her waist and pulled her against him. She didn't notice as he joined their right hands, or when he began to move in time to the music and she automatically fell in step. She didn't even hear him when he murmured her name the first time.

"Sharon?" he repeated. She looked up at him, her face pale, her eyes pools of vulnerability. "There's nothing to be upset about."

A shiver raced through her. "Did you know they would be here?"

"No, but if I had, we still would have come."

"They recognized my name."

"I doubt it." He lightly stroked her back, smoothing, soothing, trying to calm her nerves. "But even if they did, you shouldn't let it bother you. They're nice people. They wouldn't have created a scene."

"Nice? They didn't want you marrying me, and they made sure you wouldn't acknowledge that the baby was yours."

"Sharon, you took a giant leap over very shaky ground to draw that conclusion. I've already told you you're wrong to think they lied to keep us apart, or for any other reason. Now, relax."

"How many other people know about me? Does Caitlin? Am I the family joke?"

Her voice broke on the last word, and he pulled her closer. "No one knows," he said quietly. "We weren't together long enough for me to introduce you to any of the family, and only my parents knew that I was dating you and that you became pregnant."

Her lack of response didn't fool him into thinking he had pacified her. Her body was stiff, her expression distraught. He smiled gently down at her. "I can see where my parents might appear formidable to anyone who didn't know them, but I'll let you in on a little secret. They're marshmallows."

"I doubt that."

"No, it's true. When I was young, one used to protect me from the other, only neither ever figured out that the other one was doing the same thing. I can remember when I was about four or five, my father gave me strict instructions to stay out of his study. Naturally, like any other little boy, I regarded his warning as an invitation. One afternoon I decided it would be fun to play businessman. I sneaked into his study and sat at his desk and 'read' his papers. I also signed my name on every document I could find, just as I had seen my father do many times. Except, of course, I printed. But it was really *nice* printing, with good, solid, block construction of all my letters. Really, you should have seen it." For the first time, she smiled, and, encouraged, he went on. "When my mother found me, I thought my life was over. I'd never seen her so angry. But my father came in, took one look at my stricken face, and announced he had given me permission to be in there. Later, when mother left, he told me if I ever did anything like that again, he would give me a spanking I wouldn't soon forget."

"And did you? Do anything like that again?"

"Of course. I was a little boy. But he never once spanked me. Neither did Mother." He paused. "They really are nice people, Sharon."

"There's no reason for you to defend them to me," she said dully. "They protected you as a little boy and they continued protecting you as you grew older. They sound like ideal parents."

He gave a silent, colorful curse. He had meant to divert her, not remind her. Instantly he decided on another tactic. "I think I can safely say we've accomplished a great deal here tonight," he said.

Slightly wary but nevertheless curious, she asked, "And what would that be?"

"Well, for instance, you don't seem the least bit self-conscious about my holding you."

She tensed, then, realizing he was right, she slowly relaxed again. While her mind had been on other things, her body had adjusted to his.

A silence that was oddly companionable fell between them, and as they continued to dance, her gaze wandered to the other people on the dance floor. She saw Angelica DiFrenza, vivacious and full of life, her dark eyes sparkling with gaiety as she laughed up at the man with whom she danced. Then there were Caitlin and Nico, matched in strength and love, very much involved with each other. And Amarillo Smith, a man with a stillness about him even when he was moving in time to the music, a man apart, even though he was holding a gorgeous woman in his arms. Finally there were Conall's parents, standing at the edge of the dance floor, a group of people surrounding them. To her mind they all seemed larger than life; they were part of Conall's life but would never be part of hers.

Conall . . .

"Conall?"

"Yes."

"Thank you for trying to make me feel better."

It had seemed natural at the time to try to vanquish the vulnerability he had seen in her eyes, but he supposed under the circumstances he could see why she felt it unusual. "You're welcome."

"And thank you also for intervening when your mother thought she recognized my name."

Again it had seemed a natural thing for him to do, but now he realized he had been protecting her. How curious.

An incredible weariness came over Sharon all at once. The past few days had taken more out of her than she had realized, and it wasn't over yet. She leaned her head against Conall's shoulder and felt his arms bring her closer against him. The clean, spicy scent of him invaded her senses. His strength comforted and assured her. The music drifted through her mind and began to clear away the disturbing events of the evening.

She closed her eyes and remembered again the moment she had met his parents. It could have been awful, but he had chosen not to let her be humiliated and hurt. Most likely, he had only been trying to avoid a scene, but whatever his reason, she was grateful. And now she was in his arms, pressed against his body, and for the moment at least she saw no reason to leave.

Four

Sharon's breath caught in her throat as the car she was riding in rounded a curve in the long drive and suddenly she saw SwanSea.

Autumn winds were gusting, bending the tree limbs halfway to the ground, and sending brilliantly colored leaves scurrying while waves pounded into the shore. Dark brooding clouds hung low. And amid it all, the great house of SwanSea—immense and magnificent—stood on a bluff overlooking the ocean. It seemed at one moment a living force, at another a work of art.

Conall had insisted they use his private plane to fly to Maine. But when Sharon had arrived at the airport, the pilot had handed her a message from Conall saying that a business emergency prevented him from joining her until later in the evening. Her first impulse had been to wait for him, but the pilot informed her that he had specific instructions to fly her to SwanSea and then return for Conall. The plane had flown into a small airport south of SwanSea's closest town. A car and driver had been waiting for her.

And now she was there. She had read about

the house, had even seen pictures of it, but nothing had prepared her for it.

As soon as the car rolled to a stop, a tall, dignified, silver-haired gentleman came out of one of the two carved black-walnut-front doors and descended the steps. Waving aside a waiting attendant, he opened the car door for her.

"Miss Graham?" he said in a clipped British accent, helping her out. "I'm Winston Lawrence, manager of SwanSea. *Welcome.* We are so pleased you are going to be with us for a while."

"Well, thank you." She was somewhat taken aback by the personal greeting, since her usual greeting whenever she traveled was a polite request, accompanied occasionally by a smile, to sign the register.

"I hope your trip was pleasant," he said, managing to supervise the unloading of her luggage while giving her his complete attention.

The wind whipped at her, pulling free the pins that had secured her hair at the back of her head. She brushed a heavy haze of hair from her face and inhaled the tangy scent of the sea. "The trip was fine. A bit bumpy because of the weather, but very short."

"Yes, Mr. Deverell's plane certainly makes quick work of the distance between here and Boston, doesn't it? They notify us when it takes off from Logan, and then again when it lands here, so we'll have a timetable with which to work."

"I see." She didn't really, but she supposed it had something to do with the perks of being a Deverell. "Have you been informed of Mr. Deverell's delay?"

He gave a brisk nod. "Our latest word is that he will arrive sometime this evening. Now, if you'll just come this way, we'll have you settled in no time." He glanced over his shoulder at a young man dressed in a bellman's uniform. "Peter will bring your bags."

Instead of following right away, she hung back and gazed up at the house. It loomed before her with an aura of strength and indomitability. And she had the sudden, distinct impression she should proceed cautiously.

She was being absurd, she told herself in the next moment, and attempted to shake away the feeling. By the time she entered the grand entry hall, she had met with only limited success.

But everywhere she looked there was beauty.

Dominating the entry hall was a huge marble center staircase with a Tiffany stained-glass window of a peacock gracing its first landing. Above her, flower-shaped light fixtures hung on forty-foot chains from the two-story vaulted ceiling. And as a complement to the splendor and grace, harp music floated out of a nearby room, wandered in and out of the thin green leaves of the palm trees that filled the corners, and whispered across the works of art on the walls. Wide-eyed with admiration, she took everything in.

She and the manager reached the fourth floor by a private elevator tucked beneath and behind the grand staircase. There, Winston Lawrence led her to the end of a long, wide hall and ushered her into a suite.

"Mr. Deverell uses these rooms when he is with us. The suite at the other end of the hall is set aside for Mr. and Mrs. DiFrenza. The staff and I are hoping they will soon be bringing the young master for his first visit."

She blinked. "You mean their new baby?"

"Yes. SwanSea will be his one day, you know."

It was a different way of thinking, she realized, and one in which she had had no experience. Winston Lawrence was gazing expectantly at her.

"In which bedroom would you like Peter to place your things?" he asked.

"Uh, which bedroom does Mr. Deverell normally use?"

"The one to your left.'"

"Then I'll take the other."

"Very good," he said, his only expression one of a willingness to please. He motioned to Peter, and the young man vanished through a cream and gilded door with her luggage. "The staff is at your disposal, Ms. Graham. Please let us know if there is anything we can do to make your stay more enjoyable."

"Thank you very much," she said, feeling a wild desire to tip him but knowing it wouldn't be proper. She would be extra generous with Peter, she decided, but several minutes later when she tried, she met with refusal.

"We do not accept tips from the Deverells and their guests," he said with a smile. "Have a nice day."

And then she was left alone, feeling slightly shell-shocked by the place that would serve as her home for the next two weeks.

Gazing around her, she saw the sitting room of the suite was done in green, burgundy, and blue. French doors that opened out onto a terrace banked a marble fireplace carved with fluid, arabesque lines.

Out of curiosity, she made her way to the bedroom Winston Lawrence had said Conall used, and peeked in. A massive sleigh bed sat in the center of the room, covered by a royal purple spread with accent pillows of Chinese blue, deep green, burgundy, and red. A wrought-iron grapevine with leaves and twisting stems grew across the width of the wall above the bed. Springing from this fantasy grapevine were lights of different shapes and sizes, hanging like exotic blossoms. An oil painting commanded a second wall, its subjects a bare-breasted woman and the sea. The woman was partially dressed in red and gold flowing, diaphanous veils, and her long hair streamed sinuously out to blend with the sea and the veils.

The colors of the room were rich, muted, its texture sumptuous, sensual, and luxurious, its ambience unbearably erotic. She quickly left, crossed the sitting room, and opened the door to the bedroom she had chosen for herself.

This room had been done in the same colors as the other, only softer and with a sheen of iridescence. The oak and mahogany bed had been crafted with a flower-patterned marquetry of ash, satinwood, sycamore, and holly inlays. Stacked atop the lavender satin bedspread were pastel aqua and plum velvet pillows.

On a large bedside table, ten iridescent lilies, gold laid over green, drooped from gilt bronze stems—the lamp unmistakably the work of Louis Comfort Tiffany. A pearly opalescent vase filled with fresh cut orchids graced a dresser. Frieze figures of nude women encircled the vase.

The whole suite seemed to cocoon her in eroticism. It was just the art nouveau decor, she told herself.

Except there was one more thing. The obvious costliness and, in most cases, museum quality of the furnishings didn't entirely explain why she felt as if she shouldn't touch anything, perhaps, in fact, *shouldn't even stay.*

Was it SwanSea, she wondered, protecting its own? Did the great house somehow sense that if her plan were successful, there would be a child with Deverell blood running through his or her veins who would never be able to claim it as home?

She touched her forehead. "Lord, Sharon, you are really losing it," she whispered.

"And not only that you're talking to yourself."

At that moment the storm broke. Rain pounded against the windows, and overhead thunder boomed like an angry god.

She jumped, then shook her head at her foolishness. She noticed her luggage neatly stacked on the padded bench at the end of the bed and decided to unpack, grateful she had found a distraction. Assuming Conall would arrive around six, she had a few hours to put away her things and accustom herself to her surroundings.

But at seven that evening a message arrived from Conall, letting her know he wouldn't be able to make it for dinner. She frequently ate out alone, but SwanSea was having a strange effect on her, and she elected to have dinner brought to her room.

The noise of the storm eventually receded, though the rain continued. By ten o'clock she was soaking in the incredible seashell-shaped marble tub in her bathroom, trying to soothe nerves by this time strung painfully tight.

Her lips quirked at a thought. She would have felt better if she and Conall could have arrived together and gone right to bed. As it was, this wait was giving her ample opportunity to review every doubt and every fear she had ever had about her plan.

There was something wrong, something bothering her, something very important she felt she had overlooked. She just wished she could figure out what it was.

Once out of the tub, she dried off and automatically slipped her arms into her chenille bathrobe and wrapped it around her. She hadn't known what sort of clothes to bring with her, so she had brought a little of everything, including her much-loved chenille robe. Over the years it had faded from its original dark blue to a whitish-blue, and frequent washing had claimed a portion of its chenille tufts. But it was soft and warm and whenever she put it on, she felt comforted.

She could think of nothing else to do, so she went into the sitting room and spent the next couple of hours curled up on a deep-green velvet couch in front of the fire.

At midnight, when Conall finally arrived and opened the door to the suite, he found the sitting room shadowed, with light streaming into the room from the bedroom to his right, and a red-gold glow coming from embers in the fireplace.

Sharon turned.

"Did you give up on me?" he asked her, waving the luggage-laden bellboy toward the left bedroom.

"I didn't know what to think," she said truthfully. There had been moments when she'd been afraid he wouldn't come; then there'd been the fear he would.

"It was a day of problems," he said, crossing the room to sink wearily onto the couch beside her, a cushion away. "I just couldn't seem to break free."

Her senses, already deluged, strained beneath the burden of his nearness. The sensual environment of their surroundings enhanced the impact of his masculinity in spite of the fact that the lines of his face seemed harsher tonight, his skin paler. "You look tired."

He eyed her thoughtfully, then propped his elbow on the back of the couch and rubbed his forehead. "And you look tense."

"I am a little. Waiting for you here, alone, with nothing to do . . ." She shrugged.

"Didn't you get out of the suite?"

"I decided to wait. Swansea is a little overwhelming."

"Overwhelming?" He frowned. "You're not intimidated, are you?"

"I'm not sure if *intimidated* is the right word." She paused, attempting to clarify her impressions. "It's simply that I'm getting the strangest feeling, as if there's some uncertainty here about whether or not to welcome me."

His gaze sharpened. "Are you telling me the staff—"

"No, no. They've gone overboard to be hospitable. It's the *house.* Or hotel, or whatever this place is. It's *SwanSea.*"

He laughed, then abruptly groaned and increased the pressure of his fingers, rubbing them back and forth across his forehead. "I had no idea you were so impressionable."

"I'm not normally. In fact, I can't ever remember feeling this way before. Conall, are you all right? Is there something wrong?"

"No, nothing's wrong. And I'm sure once you learn to find your way around SwanSea you'll be all right. We can explore tomorrow."

If she hadn't been watching him so closely, she would have missed the wince he gave, because he quickly schooled his expression to normality. "Conall, what's wrong? Why are you rubbing your head like that?"

"I told you, it's nothing. Just a slight headache."

"Have you taken anything?"

"No. It'll go away." He dropped his hand to the back of the couch. "So, tell me, besides this very peculiar reaction you're having to the house, is everything else to your liking?"

"What's not to like? It's fabulous."

He glanced over her shoulder and saw the light streaming from the second bedroom. "You decided to use that room?"

"Mr. Lawrence told me you always take the other."

"Separate bedrooms, Sharon? That's going to make it rather difficult for you to get pregnant unless you know something I don't."

"I don't have to *sleep* with you." She made a vague gesture. "I'll go back to my room after . . . afterward." Instead of the sarcastic retort she had expected, she received a grunt. He was rubbing his temple again. "Your head really is hurting, isn't it?"

"It's nothing."

She made a disgusted sound. "Honestly! Men are either complete babies about pain or they refuse to acknowledge it. I might have known you'd be the type to refuse to acknowledge it."

"You sound like an expert on men."

"I've worked with enough over the years," she muttered, scooting across the cushion to him. "Let me see if I can help." She placed her hands at his temples and began to rub in tiny circles over his forehead, down the side of his face to the back of his neck, then returning to his forehead to repeat the process.

At first he kept his eyes shut. There was an exquisite quality to her touch as she attempted to smooth away his pounding pain. He liked the way her breath lightly fanned his face. And he enjoyed inhaling the clean, lightly floral, definitely feminine scent of her. Slowly awareness began to replace pain.

"Does your work do this to you?" she asked softly, concentrating on applying the correct amount of pressure.

He opened his eyes. "Sometimes."

"If you take into account all of the Deverell holdings, you must have thousands of employees. I can't believe out of all those people, there aren't at least a few who could take part of the burden from you." The softness of her tone carried a hint of anger.

"I have top-flight people working for me, Sharon."

"Then you must not be delegating properly."

Now she sounded as if she were scolding him. If he didn't know any better, he would think she was concerned. "I can delegate all day long," he said quietly, "but I'm still the person at the end of the chain of command. I always have to be right."

"I guess I've never thought of it in quite that way before," she murmured, giving consideration to what he said. Conall had an empire and all the benefits that went with it, but it seemed the cost of those benefits was quite high.

"You have a wonderful touch," he whispered. "It's almost worth the headache."

The intimate timbre of his whisper caused a flickering of warmth in her. She tensed, hoping to avoid a fire. "Are you feeling better?"

"Yes."

He reached out and lightly stroked his fingers down the side of her neck. "I like your robe."

She had forgotten how close she was to him or even what she had on. "It's very old." She quickly sat back.

His mouth twisted wryly. "I see there are still a few thorns."

"I beg your pardon?"

"Thorns, remember? If I tried to hold you right now, I'd get stuck and probably bleed. I guess it's the price I have to pay for leaving you alone the last five days."

"You were busy."

"Yes, I was. Besides that, it was probably best I stayed away from you until now. I couldn't have been with you without wanting to make love to you." His finger found her collarbone and lightly caressed its length. "What about you? What have you been doing for the past five days?"

Breath lodged in her throat; a mild panic set in. She had to remind herself that his question signified nothing more than casual interest. "Winding things up."

He nodded. "The company you work for has a good reputation, although we've never done business with them."

"I know." Humor sprang to life in his eyes, deepening the color of blue and catching her attention.

"Sounds like you checked it out before you went to work there."

She fought against a smile, however brief it would have been. "I did. I didn't want to be employed by a company where I might have to come into contact with you."

"But in the end you sought me out."

"For a personal reason that had nothing to do with business." She saw him wince again. "I thought you said you felt better."

"I do."

"Yeah, sure you do. I'm going to call down for aspirin."

"No, don't bother the staff."

"Bother them? I'm sure they'd gladly bring you a whole pharmacy if you asked them."

"You think so?" he asked.

Again she saw the humor glinting in his eyes, almost, she thought, as if he were enjoying being with her. "I know so."

"I'll tell you what, let's go swimming instead. It will help both my headache and your tension."

"Swimming? But it's after midnight."

"Is there something else you'd rather do?"

She thought of the alternative—staying in the suite and going to bed with him. "A swim sounds good."

"Did you bring a swimsuit?"

She nodded.

"Good, then get it, and I'll meet you back in here in a few minutes. And wear a coat. The rain has stopped and the pool house isn't very far, but it's a cool evening."

Conall was already cutting smoothly through the water when Sharon walked out of the changing room and took the ladder down into the pool. The only lights in the cavernous room came from beneath the water. They bounced illumination off the blue-tiled walls in wavering, dreamlike patterns, giving her the feeling that they were in an underwater grotto.

She struck out, her pace slow and steady. She swam the length of the pool and back again, repeating the course until her legs and arms were tired and her lungs were threatening to give out. Then she retreated to the side of the pool to watch Conall as he continued to slice through the water with strong, clean strokes, showing no signs of the fatigue she had seen in him when he first arrived.

Even as a young man he had possessed an exciting power and grace. Now his power was controlled, and his grace had turned to cool elegance. She leaned her head back against the pool's edge and acknowledged the inevitable. He was still the most exciting man she had ever known.

Suddenly he veered from his straight course and headed toward her. When he stopped, he had trapped her against the wall with a hand on either side of her head.

Water beaded on his broad, muscled shoulders and clung to the thickness of his dark eyelashes; his chest rose and fell rapidly as he drew air into his lungs. The pounding of her heart, she realized, had nothing to do with the exertion of her swim. Without doing anything overtly sexual, without touching her, he was affecting her physically, and she had to be very careful not to let him know. "Feel better?" she asked.

"My headache is completely gone."

Before she could make a light, casual reply, he leaned down and pressed a deep, wet kiss to her mouth. Her body's response was instantaneous. Her lips parted of their own volition, accepting his attention with a naturalness that frightened because she had been so absolutely set on resisting.

When he lifted his head, he skimmed his fingertips across her forehead. "How about you? Did the swim release some of that tension?"

She nodded, though she was now coping with a different kind of tension, a type in some ways infinitely more difficult to deal with. "I had to stop, though. I'm obviously not in as good shape as you are."

He cupped her breast. "There's nothing in the world wrong with the shape you're in. In fact, I find it quite alluring." His caress was light at first, then his thumb began to move back and forth and the pressure of his hand increased, molding the rounded flesh.

Beneath the thin, wet material of her swimsuit, she felt her nipples stiffen. She grabbed his wrist, trying to stop him. "You shouldn't do this. Someone might come in."

"The pool house is closed this time of night, and I took the added precaution of locking the door."

"Oh."

"Feel better about it?" His voice echoed hollowly as if to emphasize that they were the only two people there.

The pool pump was off, the water was still, all was quiet as he waited for her answer. But fighting the rising need had sapped her energies, and desire had closed her throat.

Then his hand moved, sending soft ripples through the water. He delved beneath the top of her suit, tucked its stretch material beneath her breast with a twist of his hand, and took possession of the fullness.

The sound of her gasp rebounded off the walls, parting the quiet.

"We could do anything we want here and no one would interrupt us."

They were completely isolated due to hour and place, their bodies were slick and scantily clothed, their breath rough and uneven from their laps and their growing passion. In spite of herself, their situation seemed incredibly erotic to her. That it did alarmed her. "Not here, Conall."

"Why not? It's a myth, probably made up by some teenage boy, that you can't get pregnant in a swimming pool."

"It would be better in bed," she said, grasping at straws.

"It would be fantastic in bed," he said, his voice lowering, deepening to a growl, "but I can also make it fantastic here. Trust me."

"Trust you?" she asked incredulously.

"Yes, trust me."

Suddenly he lifted her, fitting her legs around his waist, and took several turns toward deeper water. Automatically she put her arms around his neck for support. When he stopped, the weight of the water seemed greater, forcing her closer to him. And one bare breast pushed against his chest.

"I get you for two weeks," he said huskily, "and you get your chance for a baby. From your point of view, I would think the sooner we start, the better your chances would be. From my point of view, the sooner we start, the more often I can have you."

She supposed what he said made perfect sense. She wasn't sure, though, because she was having trouble thinking. In the cool, silky water, his body radiated heat to hers. And Lord, how she wanted the heat! She wanted it almost as much as she wanted better to feel the exquisite pressure of his arousal. Without considering the consequences, she wrapped her legs more tightly around him.

He edged his fingers beneath the elastic of her swimsuit bottom. "We have a deal, Sharon, and I can't wait to begin. I want you now."

The heat growing low in her body belied her words. "Now is not right."

"Why not? Is something else you want? Champagne? Moonlight? Music and flowers? I'm sure before the two weeks is over, you'll get it all."

"It's not that."

"Then what? When you talked about this deal, nothing was said about where or when."

"I know. I'm sorry. I—I've got to go back to my room." She pushed away and swam to the end of the pool.

His dark gaze followed her as she climbed out and rushed toward the dressing room, unsure why he had let her slip away from him. His muscles were coiled in readiness to go after her, but he willed himself to stay where he was.

Normally he wasn't a patient man—he didn't have to be—and he was certainly feeling anything but patient now. But almost from the first with Sharon, he had gone against his nature and allowed her to call most of the shots—at least when it came to this sexual relationship they were trying to develop.

Everything that was in him told him he could have had her, right there, right then. All it would have taken was a little more persuasion on his part. A few more kisses, a few more caresses, and she would have been his.

His face hardened, took on a more primitive cast. He would have her. It was just a matter of time.

He dove beneath the water, and when he surfaced at the other end of the pool, he turned and began swimming laps again.

Five

Despite his rigorous exercise of the night before, Conall slept fitfully and never achieved a complete state of relaxation. He woke in a bad mood, and didn't have to ask himself why. He placed an order for coffee, juice, and croissants, then dressed and walked into Sharon's bedroom.

The sunlight filtering around the edges of the curtain lightened the room and allowed him to see that she was still asleep. Quietly he opened the curtains, then stepped to the bed.

She was lying on her back, her head turned to one side, her hand beside her face, palm up. The sheet had fallen down to her waist, exposing the shimmering blue bodice of her nightgown; one thin strap had fallen off an ivory-hued shoulder. Her hair spread around her head in natural curls. As he studied her, knots of desire formed and constricted in his stomach. More than anything, he wanted to climb into bed beside her. Instead, he reached down and touched a silky brown ringlet, and remembered. . . . He had never slept the night through with her, with her head cradled against his shoulder, his body curved around hers.

He silently cursed. What the hell difference did it make? There were several women he had taken to bed with whom he had never slept the night. He turned on his heel and stalked out.

As he left, Sharon slowly exhaled. Without opening her eyes, she had felt his presence and known he was in a dark mood. His tension was so strong, it had an energy and heat all its own, and it had hit against her again and again.

She understood his tension, first of all because it was her fault, and second, because his mood exactly matched hers.

Reluctantly she opened her eyes to the sunlight and blinked. How could it be morning, she wondered, when it felt as if she had just closed her eyes. She'd tossed and turned for hours, thinking of how it had been in the swimming pool with him, her body locked against his. All through the lonely night she had pondered how easy it should have been for her to let him make love to her and wondered why it hadn't been. What in the world was wrong with her?

She seemed to be sabotaging her own plans, and for the first time she was beginning to suspect that her reasons for seeking Conall out were much more complex than she had previously admitted to herself. And if that were true, she didn't have one chance in hell of a happy ending for herself.

She heard a knock on the sitting room door, then the sound of Conall opening it and a cart being wheeled in. It was time to get up, she decided reluctantly.

Minutes later Conall glanced around as she walked into the room. The sight of her made him suck in his breath. She looked unbearably sexy with her hair wild and loose around her shoulders and her bare feet peeking beneath the ragged hem of her chenille robe. Lord, but he wanted her.

"Good, you're up," he said in an expressionless tone. "You're just in time to have a bit of breakfast and join me for a ride."

"A ride? You mean horses?"

"Yes. Have you ever ridden?"

"I had lessons when I was young, but that was so many years ago."

His shrug made light of her hesitancy. "It will all come back to you. Besides, we'll take it at a comfortable pace. It won't be a steeplechase." He glanced at his watch. "I'll wait while you eat and change. Did you pack any jeans, by the way?"

She nodded.

"Then help yourself to whatever you want," he said, indicating the table. "I'll contact the stables and have them saddle another horse."

Fallen leaves crunched beneath the hooves of the horse Sharon rode. She and Conall had taken the horses on a gallop along the cliffs, then had circled behind SwanSea to follow a path that climbed gently upward through a meadow. Yesterday's clouds had blown out to sea, leaving the air clear and crisp. Elm and aspen trees splashed bursts of vivid yellow, red, and burnt orange against a crystal-blue sky. It was a glorious day, but Sharon was miserable.

She reached down and patted the warm, damp neck of the sorrel she was riding. Conall's initial attempt at casual conversation had dwindled, then stopped, and she knew her monosyllabic responses were to blame. Somehow she had to force herself to relax or her dream of a baby of her very own would never come true.

Suddenly her horse shied as a squirrel raced

across the path in front of her. Instinctively she pulled back on the reins. The horse shook its head against the restraint, snorting loudly.

Conall quickly urged his horse up beside hers. "Take it easy. Hold him steady."

He reached out to cover her hand with his, and she started as if he'd burned her.

His face darkened. "The horse can feel your nerves, Sharon."

"Sorry."

"Forget it. Why don't we rest for a while." He scanned the meadow. "Follow me."

On a rise that offered a sweeping view of SwanSea and its surroundings, he dismounted, then came around and grasped her by the waist to help her off. Except he didn't immediately put her down. Instead, he gave in to a compulsion and continued holding her, supporting her weight so that she was caught against him, her feet inches from the ground. He held her there, just long enough to feel the length of her against him, just long enough to have the breeze send a fragrant strand of her hair to brush his face. Just long enough for her breathing to quicken. Just long enough for him to see the fever building in her eyes.

But when a curious panic began to mix with the fever, he set her on her feet and strode away to unbuckle a blanket from the rear of his saddle. He pulled the bridles from both horses and left them to graze.

She watched him, embarrassed at her panicky reaction. She waited until the color receded from her face, then bridged the silence by asking, "Won't the horses wander off?"

"They won't go far, and they'll come when I call."

"You've trained them well. The sorrel is a joy to

ride, but I'm afraid I'm going to be sore in a few hours."

"A soak in the tub should take care of that." He spread the blanket over the ground and dropped down onto it.

She sat down beside him, wondering what she could do or say to end the awkwardness between them.

An orange and gold leaf cartwheeled onto the blanket. Eager for something, anything, to do, she reached for it and idly twirled it by its stem.

The panorama before them was breathtaking, with the fiery colors of autumn everywhere, and in the far distance the ocean sparkled diamondlike. The scene that nature had landscaped was beautiful, but SwanSea still managed to dominate. Built in the shape of a giant seashell, the great stone house was at once a part of its surroundings, yet apart from it, with its own unique history, force, and strength. She couldn't imagine ever being completely comfortable in it.

"What's it like to be able to call such a house your home?" she asked, genuinely curious.

His head jerked around, as if the sound of her voice had taken him by surprise. "It's never actually been my home. I grew up in my parents' home in Boston, but I guess you could say SwanSea was my second home. I spent a lot of holidays and summers here." He gazed down at the house. "Even though I called her crazy at the time, I'm glad Caitlin brought it to life again for all of us."

"Us?"

"The family. I never tire of coming here, even with all the guests."

"Well, you can't really say the guests get in your way. You have your own private elevator, your own floor, a staff that apparently lives to serve you. You even stable your horses here."

He turned back and regarded her thoughtfully. "That's the most you've said all morning."

She shifted on the blanket as the inner tension that had been with her since she arrived began to rise again. "You haven't exactly been talkative yourself."

"At least I tried."

"Well, I'm trying now. Okay?"

"Okay. So why are you sitting so far away from me?"

She gave a nervous laugh. "I'm not. I mean, this blanket isn't big enough for me to be *too* far away."

He gazed pointedly at the wide space between them, then back at her. "See, Sharon, it's this way. In most circles I'm considered quite bright, but I'm having a hell of a time figuring you out."

She pulled her knees up to her chest and wrapped her arms around her legs. "There's no need for you to figure me out."

"You're very wrong," he said, his voice as quiet and as cool as a frost-covered morning. "You want me to get you pregnant. I want you, period. Now, on the surface those two goals would seem compatible, but your signals to me are so mixed, I'm beginning to wonder if . . ."

"What?"

"I'm beginning to doubt if this deal we made is going to work out."

Her chest tightened with fear. Had she messed things up so badly that he was thinking of backing out? It seemed as if that was just what she had done. Even worse, she knew exactly what he was talking about. Ever since she'd been at SwanSea, her emotions had been spinning out of control, and she'd been acting little better than a tease, giving in to him one minute, pulling away the next.

"Have you changed you mind, Sharon? You don't want to try this after all?"

"No, no, it's not that."

"Then I don't understand," he said, turning to her, frustration heavily lacing his voice. "What is it you want? Is it the moonlight and roses I mentioned last night? Or do you want to get reacquainted before we go to bed?"

She shook her head, growing more and more miserable. "Of course not. This is a business deal."

"That's what you keep saying," he snapped, "but business deals require good faith on both sides, and so far, sweetheart, I've seen very little good faith on your part."

"We've been here only twenty-four hours!"

"And we have only two weeks!" He snatched up a pebble from the ground and hurled it as far as he could.

Her heartbeat sounded like thunder in her ears. "Look, it's just that this is a little harder than I imagined it would be."

"Why? It's not as if I make your skin crawl. The couple of times we've kissed, I can tell that your instinct is to respond. Unfortunately, somewhere along the line, something gets in the way. What is it? *Talk to me.*"

A hurting pressure was building inside her. It felt as if he were scratching at her flesh, trying to expose something she didn't want uncovered.

"Dammit, Sharon, is all this deliberate? Is this your way of punishing me?"

"*No!*" Pain filled her eyes as she gazed at him. "No," she said more softly. "No, I'm not trying to punish you."

"Then what?"

She stared toward the distant horizon, but what she saw was a picture of a frightened young girl. "That night, ten years ago, after you came to me and told me the baby I was carrying couldn't be yours, I went to a park and sat on a bench for hours."

"By *yourself*? But it must have been ten, eleven o'clock."

"I sat there," she said as if she hadn't heard him, "and cried until I couldn't cry anymore. And then I thought of ways of getting even with you. Finally, I went home and told my parents I was pregnant, but that the father of the baby wouldn't acknowledge that it was his. I watched my mother go pale and my father turn and walk out of the room, and I came up with more ways of getting even with you. The night I lost my baby and I was lying on a gurney in a drafty hall of the hospital, all alone, bleeding, and in so much pain I thought I would die, I tried to come up with something that would be bad enough to do to you then too." Her words came to a halt as her throat clogged and her body shuddered.

She glanced at him. She had his complete attention. "My father never spoke to me again because he believed your story over mine. From that point on he washed his hands of me. Whenever my mother and I wanted to see each other, we had to meet somewhere other than the house. When he died, I went to his funeral, stared at his coffin, and thought about how I had lost him years earlier. Once again I made plans to get even with you."

He was staggered at how much she had been through and shocked that he had never considered it before. As hellish as that time had been for him, it had been just as bad or worse for her. And she'd gone through it alone. He felt a stab of guilt. "I had no idea, Sharon."

Her lips curved slightly. "How could you know?

You graduated from college, took your place in the business world and in society, and never looked back. My story is quite different. For several years afterward, in between the hours I spent at school and work, I tried to come up with the ultimate revenge against you, but I never could. Then you know what? One day I simply gave up. And just so there'll be no lingering doubt in your mind, I'll say it one more time. No, this is not my way of punishing you."

"Okay," he said slowly, "so then what is it you want?"

She didn't hesitate. "I want a baby."

"But—and I want to be absolutely clear on this—you don't want just any baby, you want *my* baby. Right?"

"Yes."

"Because when and if that happens, you will have your vindication." When a brief expression of puzzlement crossed her face, he added, "That's what you said in my office."

She nodded. "I want exoneration. If I get pregnant, it will by my proof that I was telling the truth all those years ago . . . even though there's no one left alive who cares but me."

A sudden feeling of helplessness washed over him. What could he say to her? All this time, when he had thought of that awful night he had confronted her with his sterility, he had remembered only the big hole she had left in his gut when she had turned and run out of his apartment. For the first time he had to look at that night and their situation from her perspective.

"I'm sorry you had to go through all of that. I should have tried to help."

"You didn't think it was your responsibility," she said, understanding that he still wasn't admitting he'd been wrong.

"Nevertheless, we were close, even it it was only for a few months. If I hadn't felt so betrayed . . ." He trailed off, then after a moment started again. "If we hadn't been so damned young . . ." He shrugged. "At the very least, you should have had help." He grimaced. "Dammit, how could your father believe a stranger over his own child?"

If by some miracle he were ever lucky enough to have a child of his own, he thought, he would always be there for him, always believe him. But a child of his own was an impossibility he tried never to think about. Maybe someday he would adopt.

"Once I told him who you were, it was quite easy for him to believe you. Deverell is a well-known name worldwide, and in New England it's right up there with the pope."

"You're exaggerating."

"You know better than that," she chided him. "Especially now that your uncle is running for president. And back then, when I told my father you were a Deverell, he was ecstatic. He saw it as a chance to be connected to a great family. Then I told him you were denying that the baby was yours and why, and he saw his chance evaporate. He railed at me for messing up what he saw as an opportunity of a lifetime. He also called me a slut for sleeping with two men at the same time." Her voice wavered, but she quickly regained her control. "I think that's about the last thing he ever said to me."

"He must have been some kind of monster!"

"No, just a man who had worked hard all his life and wanted something better for both himself and his family."

"He was your *father*. He should have believed you!"

"Yes, he should have," she said quietly. "And so should you."

"That was different, and you know it."

"Was it?"

She brushed a strand of hair from her face and remembered that she hadn't bothered to blow it free of curls this morning so that it would hang straight. Then she remembered how for years she'd carried her pain closed up inside her. Now she'd exposed a part of it to him, getting it out of her system, and in doing so, perhaps even managing to transfer a small part of the burden. *It felt good.*

Conall finally broke the silence. "There's a lot between us, Sharon, maybe too much for us to continue with this. If you'll give this deal a real hard look, you'll see it's pretty simplistic."

A chill gripped her, bringing with it panic and an unexplainable fear. "I didn't tell you all of that to make it impossible for us, Conall."

"Maybe not, but—"

She held out her hands in unconscious entreaty. "It was very hard for me to come to you, Conall, and ask you to make me pregnant, but I did it. I'll get over this too."

"Get over *what*?"

She dropped her hands. Maybe it was time to tell him one more thing. "Don't laugh," she said softly.

"Laugh! We'll both be damned lucky if I don't cry!"

She was diverted. "You? I don't believe it."

"I've acquired multimillion-dollar companies with less trouble than this."

"You're *not* acquiring me."

He sighed heavily and rubbed his eyes. "I didn't mean to imply that I was. Just tell me what in the hell else is going on here."

A sudden brief rush of wind sent leaves scattering across the meadow. Her eyes followed their path. "I haven't been deliberately teasing you, Conall. Perhaps it's as you say. I took too simplistic a view. I thought this out as a business deal, and now I'm having trouble with the concept of going to bed with you in what would be only an emotionless encounter. Silly, isn't it?"

Revelation upon revelation, he thought, staring at her. She wasn't as cold-blooded about this as she had tried to make him think. "What kind of emotion is it that you want?" he asked, calmer now that he understood her a little better.

Emotion was exactly what she was having trouble with. She skittered away from the idea and went another way with her thoughts. "Maybe I need to feel a little more at ease. Going to bed with you after all these years is going to require—" What? she wondered. Surely she wasn't so foolish as to want *love*. That would be supreme stupidity on her part. "Look, I know you view this as simply a two-week roll in the hay, but—"

"You're going to have to trust me on this, Sharon, but I have never in my life viewed any sexual encounter with a woman as a roll in the hay."

His dry tone made her smile, and much to her astonishment she realized that though neither of them had moved, he seemed closer. Was her mind playing tricks on her? Or had talking this out really helped her in more ways than she had thought?

"Having a baby is the most important thing in my life, Conall. Please don't back out on me."

Something softened in him. He didn't think he'd ever seen an expression as vulnerable as hers. And gazing at her, with her face free of makeup, her hair blowing gently around her head, he could think of nothing he'd like better than to take her to bed.

But now there seemed to be so much more involved than passion. As much as she had told him, he had the feeling she had scarcely allowed him beneath the surface.

It was true they had made a connection with this conversation, and with it, inadvertently taken a giant step away from her original cut and dried proposition. He didn't know whether that was good or bad. And he had to wonder where they were going—after all, their time together would be so short.

His goal was still to get her out of his system, to make love to her until he didn't want to anymore. But the intimacy of lovemaking with him was frightening her for some reason, and he didn't want to force her.

He also didn't know how much longer he could wait for her.

He exhaled on a long breath, then smiled. "Oh, what the hell." He stood, extended his hand to her, and pulled her to her feet. "Let's go back for lunch."

From their table by a window in the dining room, Conall glanced over his shoulder, saw nothing out of the ordinary, then gazed back at Sharon. "What in the world have you been looking at for the last half hour? I'm beginning to think I'm eating alone."

She took a last spoonful of clam chowder, then pushed the delicate Spode bowl an inch or two toward the center of the linen-covered table. "I've been watching the dining room staff. They're hovering like tiny little helicopters around you and this table." As if to prove her point, a waiter appeared and whisked her soup bowl away.

"Tiny little helicopters? Come on, I haven't noticed anything unusual."

"That's just it. They hover *unobtrusively*."

A smile tugged at the corners of his mouth. "You're making that up."

"No, really. I'm fascinated."

He shrugged. "Well, thanks to Caitlin and Winston Lawrence, the staff is very well trained. Winston, being British, trained them in the European manner."

"They are well trained, and the service for the other guests is impeccable. But when it comes to you, the staff is practically standing on their toes in fear they might miss some slight sign you need something."

His smile broadened. "Now I know you're making it up. I've never noticed that I received any special attention."

"That's because they're unobtrusive about it and because you're a Deverell. You're used to the treatment they give you." She sat back in her chair, realizing with something of a shock that she was actually enjoying herself. "And they give you that treatment *because* you're a Deverell. They seem to be almost feudal in the way they view your family."

He chuckled. "I don't believe you for a minute."

"Okay, I'll prove it to you." She lifted a hand and immediately two waiters almost tripped over themselves to get to the table.

The waiter who arrived first said, "May I help you?"

"Yes, I would like a cup of coffee and Mr. Deverell would like dessert."

The eager young man turned toward Conall. "Shall I bring the dessert cart?"

"That won't be necessary," she answered before Conall could reply. "Do you have fresh raspberries?"

"SwanSea has its own hothouse that produces our fruit," he said with obvious pleasure.

"In that case, Mr. Deverell would like a bowl of fresh raspberries with a small pitcher of cream."

"Right away," the waiter said, already turning away.

"There's just one thing."

The waiter turned back. "Yes?"

"He'd like the bumps taken off the raspberries."

"The bumps?"

She leaned forward and dropped her voice to a confiding tone. "It's his digestive tract. He can't tolerate them."

The waiter looked at Conall. "I'm sorry to hear that, sir. I'll have your order out as soon as possible."

Once more he went to turn away; once more she stopped him. "I wonder if I might place our order for lunch tomorrow. It's for something special that I'm sure you don't normally have on hand."

The waiter straightened with pride. "We'd be glad to prepare any dish to your exact specifications."

"That's wonderful. You see, I developed a fondness for black-eyed peas when I was in the South last year on business and I'd like Mr. Deverell to be able to experience them for himself. I would, however, like the black eyes cut from all the peas."

The young man didn't hesitate. "Very good, Ms. Graham. Is there anything else?"

"Just one last thing. Could you please arrange to have M&M's placed in Mr. Deverell's suite, separated by color. It's his digestive system again. It's not good to mix the colors."

"I'm sure you're right." He turned to Conall. "And I'll be glad to see to that for you." With a brief half bow he left the table.

Sharon's expression was one of triumph as she looked at Conall.

His elbow was propped on the arm of the chair, the side of his face cradled in his hand, a finger pressed across his lips to keep him from laughing. "Black-eyed peas with the black eyes cut out?" he asked in amused disbelief.

"Pretty good, huh?"

"Do you have any idea how long it will take them to de-eye a pot of peas?"

She laughed. "I have a pretty good idea, but tomorrow, when we come in to lunch, I'll bet we have exactly what I ordered. And within an hour I'm sure we'll have the M&M's in the suite."

"Did you *have* to blame it on my digestive system?"

"You're right. They'll probably post a doctor in a chair outside the suite just in case you have some sort of attack. I guess I should have simply let them believe you are a true eccentric."

"I'm sure they're going to think that anyway." He infused his words with resignation, but he was teasing. He had been delighted by her little performance for the waiter. It was an indication that a part of the eighteen-year-old girl he had known and loved was still inside her. She had been full of fun and life, then. If only . . .

"Want to make a small bet on the raspberries?" she asked.

"Sure. I'll bet you a dollar that any minute now someone will come out here and tell me that what you've asked for is impossible."

"A dollar? You're a real big spender, aren't you? Make it two dollars."

"Done."

A waiter glided up to the table and set the coffee Sharon had ordered in front of her. "Your raspberries will be out in just a few minutes, Mr. Deverell. The chef asked me to apologize for the delay."

Conall somehow managed a straight face. "That's quite all right."

True to the waiter's words, a bowl of fresh raspberries, completely free of bumps, soon sat on the table in front of him, the raspberries bearing a strong resemblance to ruby-red mush. He dug into his pocket, pulled out his billfold, and handed Sharon two dollars.

"Thank you very much," she said, noticing and reacting to the twinkle in his eyes with an erratic pulse.

"Want to bet three dollars on the black-eyed peas tomorrow?"

She nodded gravely. "My faith and money is on the staff."

He reached across the table and grasped her hand, and was extraordinarily pleased when she didn't pull away. "You seem to be feeling more at ease here at SwanSea. Are you?"

"Somewhat," she said. His hand was warm over hers, and in some strange way, reassuring. She gazed around the dining room, taking in the jewellike, flower-shaped chandeliers that hung from the ceiling and the elegant table settings. "I'm awestruck by the beauty here, but . . ." Her shoulders rose and dropped. "This house has a definite personality. I'm staying here with a Deverell and therefore the house should automatically accept me, but I don't think it does." She smiled ruefully at him. "You think I'm really odd, don't you?"

He grinned. "It's a possibility I've considered."

Since she felt much the same way, she couldn't fault his attitude. Pretending to be annoyed, she tried to pull her hand away, but he held on tight.

"Look, Sharon, SwanSea was a house, now it's a hotel. You're making it sound as if it has a personality. As far as I know, Caitlin is the only other person who has ever personified SwanSea, and I think that's because she rambled around this place pretty much all alone for the first six years of her life."

"Are you telling me you've never felt anything special here?"

"No. Except . . . well, I've always felt good being here. In fact, sometimes it's hard for me to leave." Her smile told him he had just proved her point. He exhaled. "Okay, okay, so any idea why the house doesn't accept you?"

"You're going to laugh."

"I won't laugh."

"Are you sure?"

"I'm sure."

"It's almost as if it thinks I plan to harm you."

He laughed loudly. "And do you?"

"I've told you everything I plan." *Or almost everything.* "Eat your raspberries. Two waiters and a chef are hovering in that doorway over there."

He brought the back of her hand to his lips and kissed her, and she felt a tingle all the way to her toes.

"All right, but after I finish I'm going to show you a different view. The more you see of SwanSea, the sooner you'll become used to it."

* * *

"We'll go out here." Conall opened the attic window, threw one leg over the window ledge, and sat straddling it. He glanced back at Sharon and grinned. "I took a survey one summer when I was eight and decided that this window is the best one to use to climb out on the roof. The slope is fairly gentle on this part of the roof, and it leads to one of the walks."

"Eight? Did your parents know what you were doing?" She could almost see him as a young boy, his face set with determination, secretiveness, and delight as he climbed out this window to the roof to play and perhaps to dream of the man he would become.

And, if they conceived a son here at SwanSea, she had to wonder if he would possess that engaging streak of mischievousness his father had obviously had as a boy, and much to her amazement obviously *still* had.

"Of course they didn't know." He grinned. "There are some things parents are better off not knowing. They live longer that way."

"I'm not sure I agree."

His grin widened. "I don't think my mother would either. Are you coming?"

"Are you sure this is what you want to do? We're awfully high up."

He laughed. "You noticed that, did you? Well, don't worry. I've done this many times before."

"But lately? Have you done it lately? After all, you're not as young as you once were."

His eyes narrowed. "I'm going to have to get you for that."

She giggled.

A woman would have to be dead not to respond to him, Sharon thought, secretly taking in the way he looked in his jeans and natural-colored cable knit sweater. Sexy, masculine, virile, and desirable were a few adjectives that sprang to mind. If she needed proof that she was a long way from dead, she had it. Everything that was in her was responding to him at this moment.

Since they had left the meadow, he had been a relaxed, charming companion. She had even felt comfortable kidding with him over lunch. But she had moments when it was difficult for her to reconcile this charming, playful man with the one who had hurt her so badly. And more than likely the fact that he *was* the same man made her feel guilt when she did respond to him.

He held out his hand to her. "Come on, Sharon. You don't want me to call you a chicken, do you?"

"Let me get this straight. You, Conall Jacob Deverell, whom some call brilliant, the CEO of Deverell Industries, want to climb out on a very high roof like you did when you were eight years old, and you want me to go with you?"

"That about sums it up. Are you coming?"

"Yes. Just tell me what to do."

She discovered with surprise that SwanSea's roof was a series of valleys and peaks, part shingle, part ridged copper. Pathways and steps had been laid out between the different sections to make it easier to work on. She lost count of the chimneys. She also lost her sense of direction until he led her onto a fairly flat section that overlooked the back gardens.

"Here we are," he said, dropping to sit on the sun-warmed copper, aged to a lovely green patina, and tugging her down beside him.

Below them, box hedges marched in lines that had been drawn long ago, enclosing hundreds of types of plants and flowers. In the center of the garden, myriad streams of water gracefully arced into the air, then fell into the basin of a huge marble fountain.

"It's beautiful," she murmured. "You can see forever up here."

He lifted his hand and pointed toward a distant rise on the horizon. "That's where we were this morning."

She nodded. "I don't see many people. There's a couple in the garden, another over there by the trees. I imagined SwanSea would be booked to capacity most of the time."

"It is. It's just that this time of year, during the day, most of the guests pile in their cars and take drives to see the fall leaves. Tonight, I'm sure the dining room will be filled." He glanced at her. "Would you like to take a drive tomorrow?"

"Maybe," she murmured. Tomorrow seemed so far away. "Conall, do you ever see Mark Bretton anymore?" The question had popped into her head, and she was as astonished as he to hear it.

He stiffened. "No."

"Why not? You used to be such good friends."

"The minute I found out he'd been seeing you behind my back, he ceased to be my friend."

"He wasn't seeing me. We never once went out. He tried, but I wouldn't have anything to do with him. Eventually he gave up and turned his efforts to poisoning you against me." She paused. "I never figured out if he really wanted me, or if he was jealous of you because you appeared to have it all and he wanted desperately to be able to take something you valued away from you."

Conall was silent for a moment. "I nearly killed him."

"What?"

"You told me what you did that night after you ran out of my apartment. Now I'll tell you what I did. I went to him, called him every name in the book, then proceeded to beat the living hell out of him. If someone hadn't pulled me off him, I would have killed him."

"What became of him?"

"Last I heard, he was living in Europe."

Conall had been very wrong to think that she would go to bed with his friend, she reflected, but nevertheless she saw now that he'd been deeply hurt. A person had to bear an enormous amount of pain in the course of his life. To hurt for the wrong reason and without real cause seemed to her a special kind of tragedy.

"All of a sudden I'm very tired," she murmured.

"Lie back and take a nap."

"Here?"

"Sure, why not?" The corner of his mouth curved slightly upward. "I won't let you fall."

The bed in her room was a long way away, and the idea of resting here strongly tempted her. She lay back and shut her eyes. Gradually the sun began to warm her bones, relax her muscles, clear her mind. Sometime later she felt Conall lean over her and press a soft, gentle kiss on her mouth. The kiss seemed to hold an incredible sweetness, an incredible regret. What were they to do, she wondered as she felt him lie down beside her. What were they to do. . . .

When she next opened her eyes, the sun was much lower in the sky, and Conall was standing at the edge of the roof, his arms crossed over his chest, his feet planted wide apart, staring off into the distance.

She sat up and grimaced when her muscles rebelled with pain. "Conall?"

He walked back to her, happier now that she was awake. He'd felt a peculiar kind of restlessness and aloneness while she slept. "More rested now?"

"Yes. Sorry, I didn't mean to nap so long."

"Don't worry about it. I slept too." He extended his hand. "Grab hold and I'll help you up."

She let out a groan as he pulled her to her feet. "Oh, Lord, I was afraid of this. I was still too long, and that horse ride this morning has caught up with my body."

"We'll go back in, and you can take a good long soak in the tub. I guarantee it will help."

"How do you know?"

He smiled. "I know from experience. I don't get a chance to ride unless I'm here, and I don't get here very often. I plan a soak myself."

She returned his smile, and suddenly he couldn't tear his gaze away from her. Her eyes seemed a deep, endless aqua. It would have been so easy, so natural for him to invite her into his tub. Just the thought made his muscles tighten. Heaven help him, he did *want* her.

His eyes lowered to the softness of her mouth. It was curved with amusement, as if she didn't quite believe that he was also sore. For some crazy reason he found her expression irresistible, and without further thought he angled his head down and kissed her lightly, a mere brushing of lips against lips. He hadn't meant to prolong the kiss, but once he had started he couldn't seem to stop. He tried to keep the kiss easy, but an unexpected heat flooded him, hitting his system with force. Then her arms crept around his waist, and her mouth opened. He couldn't refuse the invitation. With a rough sound he thrust his tongue deeply into her mouth and tasted his own pleasure, his own passion.

She was aching, a warm, languid kind of ache that made her want to do things slowly, but at the same time there was an urgency inside her that made her want instant gratification. She slid her hands beneath the sweater to the smooth flesh of his back and pressed herself more firmly to him.

Her breasts had begun to swell, her nipples harden. What was happening to her? Had she slept away her inhibitions with her nap? Or, more likely, had their talk this morning, plus their playful banter during lunch, begun the melting of the things that had been making her hold herself away from him? She wasn't sure. And somehow she felt it wasn't really important that she know the answer right that minute.

He understood more now, Conall thought. And amazingly he desired her more, with an intense, hot pleasure that was unfamiliar to him. His head was swimming dizzyingly. A fever had begun to burn inside him, and he had never felt better in his life. She was springtime in his arms, burgeoning with life and passion.

But he couldn't allow himself to pressure her, he wouldn't. Last night she had left him. Today he was going to have to force himself to leave her, because if he didn't, he'd never forgive himself. She had to be ready to make love; she had to want him as much as he wanted her.

Unable to pull slowly away from her, he jerked his head up, then stepped back. She was left swaying unsteadily on her feet, her eyes heavy-lidded, an expression of bewilderment on her face. He almost drew her back into his arms, then he almost took her down to the rooftop with him.

"We'll both feel better after a good hot soak," he muttered huskily, and reached out for her hand to lead her back inside.

Six

A crystal, bell-like sound rang out as Conall and Sharon touched their wineglasses together.

"To a wonderful stay here at SwanSea," he said. "May it fulfill each of our expectations."

"Now, there's a toast," she commented. "How long did it take you to come up with it?"

He lifted his hand and snapped his fingers, demonstrating the amount of time it had taken, and three waiters came running. His expression turned rueful, and Sharon laughed.

"False alarm, gentlemen," he said.

Sharon smiled and sipped her wine. The nap on the roof had left her rested, the kiss she and Conall had shared had left her a trifle off balance, yet feeling very much alive. She had no idea what would happen this evening. At this point she wasn't even sure what it was she wanted to happen. She just knew that sharing the burden with the person she had held responsible for her pain all these years had helped in some incalculable way, and she no longer felt as emotionally fragile as she once had.

As she had soaked in the seashell-shaped tub, she'd even considered a radical idea: Perhaps going to bed with Conall to conceive a child had not been such a good idea. Perhaps she should return home in the morning and continue on with her life.

And as for this evening, she had decided to take it a minute at a time, and if that proved too arduous, she would try seconds.

"How are all your aches and pains?" he asked, studying her.

"Great. You were right. The hot water soaked them all away."

"Good, then you'll be up for a little more exercise tonight."

Instinctively, involuntarily, she tensed. Then she noticed the glint of amusement in his eyes. He was teasing her, deliberately being provocative. She relaxed and gave him a melting smile. "That all depends. What kind of exercise did you have in mind?"

"You'll see." He grinned, taking great enjoyment in the simple act of sitting across the table from her and watching the different expressions that chased across her face. She looked exquisite in the evening gown she wore. The bodice had been created out of tiny iridescent beads in colors of ice, purple, turquoise, and green. The long, flowing skirt was made of sheer layers of turquoise, green, and white chiffon. She looked very cool, very seductive. In many ways, very untouchable. He wanted desperately to touch her. "Your dress is lovely. Is it new?"

"No, I've had it for about two years."

"Where have you worn it?"

She tilted her head, puzzled. "Various functions and parties. I can't remember exactly. Why?"

"I just wondered." His gaze dropped to the tantalizing shadow of her cleavage revealed by the low neckline of the dress, then returned to her face, where the ice-crystal earrings she wore were throwing light onto her skin. "Your social schedule must be quite full. Dates, I mean."

She had dated often enough over the years, she reflected. Twice she had even tried very hard to become serious. Somehow, though, the relationships had never worked out. By choice, her dates had tapered off, until now, right at this moment, she would be hard pressed to recall when she last had been out with a man. However, she had no intention of telling him any of this. "Do you honestly think my life has stood still for the last ten years?" she asked, half amused, half censorious. "Yours hasn't. Why should mine?"

"No particular reason." He picked up his wineglass, looked at it, then set it back down without drinking anything.

"Are you aware of the odd glances you're getting from the staff?" she asked.

His lips twisted with dry humor. "No, but if I am, it's your fault."

"They'll forgive you anything. Trust me."

"Should I?"

His question was asked in a teasing tone, but her answer would have been a serious, *no, not entirely*. So she remained silent and soon their dinner arrived.

"Did you notice the different bowls of M&M's in the suite?"

He nodded and smiled. "You're really something."

She felt a flutter in her heart and knew why. She was acutely aware of Conall and how darkly handsome and sophisticated he looked tonight. His coal-black hair gleamed with health and vitality. The contrast of his bronze skin against the white shirt was potently attractive. His hands especially fascinated her, with their strong wrists and long, lean fingers.

He handled the crystal wineglass with care. How would he handle a woman?

Her head came up with a snap. He was watching her watch him. A blush rushed up her neck and her hand flew to cover the telltale color.

He eyed the color with interest. "How is your salmon?"

"Wonderful," she said, grateful for the opportunity to change the direction of her thoughts. "In fact, everything about the dinner is perfect, including the ambience. If you were to discount the modern clothing worn by the guests here tonight, we could well be a hundred years back in time. The ladies dining here this evening would be wearing patterned silk or embroidered velvet gowns, with the skirts flared in back to form a short train. Or if this were the twenties, there would be flappers in short, beaded chemises, perhaps shocking the older women by smoking."

Her gaze traveled around the room. What kind of love stories had been played out between these walls, she wondered. What kind of stories would be played out in the future?

He pulled her back to the present by reaching across the table and taking her hand. "How did someone with your imagination ever choose accounting as a career?"

"That's easy. I could make sense out of numbers. You either add, subtract, multiply, or divide them, and they're either black or red. There aren't many things in life that are that simple."

"No, I suppose not." He wondered if she knew how telling her explanation was. She'd chosen a career she could control because there had been so much in her life she hadn't been able to control.

He squeezed her hand. "Are you finished with dinner?"

It was the twinkle in his eye more than the question that gave her pause. "Yes, why?"

"For our after-dinner exercise."

"Oh."

Her doubtful tone made him laugh. "I have no idea what you're thinking, but if for some odd reason you're worrying, stop it. I have a surprise for you, and I can guarantee that you're going to love it."

He glanced at one of the waiters, and in moments the young man was there with her velvet evening cloak. She had brought it with her from Boston, but had left it hanging in her room.

"I sent someone for it," Conall explained, rising and taking it from the waiter. He held out his hand to help her up, then wrapped the velvet around her shoulders and drew her back against him. "We're not going far," he murmured close to her ear.

A thrill rippled through her, and she twisted her head to look up at him.

He bent his head to press his lips to her cheek. "Let's go."

They left the house by a back door and walked out into a night glazed silver by the moon and spun with a special enchantment. The fountain was lit by colored lights and flowers scented the air.

They made their way along the winding garden paths, drawing farther and farther away from the house. But the music from the house wove in and out of the flowers, trees, and shrubs, following them.

"You've completely mystified me," she murmured, "but I'm enjoying the walk."

"I am too. It's a beautiful night, and I have a beautiful companion." He glanced at her. "I'm almost sorry we're nearly there."

"Nearly *where*?"

"You'll see."

"You said that before."

Mid-stride, he pivoted and suddenly she was in his arms, and he was kissing her. She was taken unawares. He was molding her mouth with his, drawing from her a response that came from a place inside her she hadn't known existed, a place filled with emotions that raged and yearnings that blazed. She was shocked at the hunger she felt, at the bone-deep need, at the sensual pain that had begun to throb low and hard in her stomach. Then the kiss ended as abruptly as it began.

He cradled the side of her face with one hand, and stared enigmatically down at her. Her pulses raced furiously, but she remained quiet beneath his hand, not so much waiting, not so much trying to make sense of what had just happened, but, rather, regaining her strength. After a long moment he kissed her again, more softly this time. Heat flared from the still-burning embers of their first kiss, then died back down as he took her hand and drew her around a tall hedge. Obviously he had far greater control of himself than she had of herself.

"Here we are," he said, waving a hand toward a long, narrow, one-story building with floor-to-ceiling arched windows spaced evenly down its side.

"What is it?" she whispered, still trying to deal with the effects of their kisses.

He drew a key from his pocket and unlocked the door. "It's a tennis court my grandfather, Jake, had built sometime in the twenties after he inherited SwanSea." He ushered her in with a hand at the small of her back.

The interior of the building lay in complete darkness except for the moonlight that slanted through each of the windows and sliced a short distance through the blackness.

"Stay here," Conall said, "I'll be right back."

She heard his footsteps as he walked away from her. For a moment she felt strangely bereft, but soon light flooded the interior—a subdued, pearlized kind of light—and she blinked as her mind slowly adjusted to what she was seeing.

A glass roof curved above them, artistically constructed of metal supports and pale yellow and cream stained glass.

Floor lamps stood around the perimeter of the court, the lamps each identical to the other. Each was crafted from copper and iridescent ivory glass in the shape of a tall, single-stemmed flower. On a lower leaf, a dragonfly rested.

Placed among the tall flower lamps were deep, wide, rattan couches, chairs, and chaise longues bearing cream-colored cushions. Glass-topped tables awaited cool drinks, and beside them the leaves of the potted palms stirred gently in the breeze that drifted in from both the doorway and several open windows. In the iridescent light the court resembled an enchanted garden.

"It's fantastic," she said when he returned to her side.

"I was hoping you'd like it. Since there's only one court here, Caitlin decided to place it off limits for the guests. There are outdoor courts for them, but only the family can use this one. Would you like to play?"

"Play—tennis—now?" She glanced down at her evening gown. "In these clothes?"

"Why not? And I know you play. I can remember at least a couple of games you and I played all those years ago."

He bent and pressed a light kiss on her mouth that took her mind completely off her ability to play tennis. He was kissing her more and more, she reflected. It seemed she had no more thorns.

"The light's not the best at night, but I think we can manage. Are you up to it?"

A bouncy rendition of Cole Porter's "Let's Fall in Love" drifted through the windows on the breeze along with a few gold and red leaves. This place wasn't of the real world, she thought. "Sure," she said. "I've never lived in an F. Scott Fitzgerald novel before. It should be fun."

He strode toward a cabinet at the back of the building, stripping off his jacket and tie as he went and unbuttoning the top few buttons of his shirt. When he came back, he handed her a racquet and two balls. "Your serve."

She took her position behind the baseline, tossed up the ball, and hit it as hard as she could. It landed outside the receiving court.

"Oh, too bad," Conall called in mock sympathy.

"Yeah, sure." She unbuckled her belt to give her more mobility and tossed it behind her. This time her serve landed squarely in his left serving court and the game was on.

She soon kicked off her shoes, but the full pale-turquoise skirts of her evening gown swirled and flared with her every movement and proved a definite problem. She had to lift the chiffon with one hand and swing the racquet with the other.

Still, Sharon surprised herself by holding her

own with Conall. And even when she realized that at times he was deliberately sending her easy returns, she decided she was having too much fun to care about her pride, if she'd ever had any in the first place.

Sometime later she hit a dropshot just over the net. He ran for it, but missed.

She laughed. "I win!"

His racquet clattered as it landed on the court where he tossed it in playful disgust. "*This* set you win. But the next—"

"Next?" she exclaimed, sweeping the back of her hair up so that air could reach her neck. "You've got to be kidding. No, no, no. I'm retiring as champion." She made her way off the court to a couch, where, one at a time, she propped her feet on its cushion to examine the damage she had done to her stockings. A glance confirmed what she'd already known. They were in shreds. Conall had gone over to the cabinet, so as quickly as possible, she reached beneath her long skirt to her garter belt, unhooked the stockings, and peeled them off.

A minute later he was there with two towels, and he handed her one. "I think we need to talk about this decision of yours," he said, taking up the conversation where they had left it. "A champion doesn't simply retire, you know. He, or she, as the case may be, usually takes on the most qualified challenger."

She smiled sweetly at him and patted her neck with the towel. "If I find a qualified challenger, I'll think about it."

He snatched her towel from her hands and threw both their towels aside. Then with a menacing growl he grabbed her to him. "Say you're sorry, or I'll be forced to do something drastic!"

She giggled. "Like what?"

"Are you going to say you're sorry?"

"No, I don't think so."

"Then hang on, because I'm going to have to resort to making you so dizzy you won't know which way is up or which way is down." With that, he lifted her off her feet and whirled her around and around until she was squealing with laughter. When he lowered her feet to the ground, he kept his arms around her. "Now will you say you're sorry?"

She shook her head and clung to him, unable to stop laughing or regain her balance.

He smiled broadly. "That's too bad, because, unfortunately, the longer you refuse to cooperate, the worse the torture gets." He swept her into his arms and laid her on the many cream-colored cushions of one of the rattan couches.

The next thing she knew he was braced over her, his eyes alight with laughter. "I really hate to do this," he whispered, his tone one of regret, his expression showing exactly the opposite, "but now I have to resort to the dreaded Kiss Torture."

Choking on a laugh, she drew a breath and released it unevenly. "It sounds awful."

"It is, believe me. But just close your eyes and try to bear up as best you can."

With a wide smile, she closed her eyes, expecting more fun.

She felt his lips brush like a warm, soft breeze over her forehead, then press gently against each of her eyelids. Little by little her breathing quieted.

His tongue lightly licked the bridge of her nose. Next he laid down a line of meticulously placed kisses to the tip. Her urge to laugh subsided.

With his mouth hovering just over hers, he asked, "Are you ready to say you're sorry?"

Her smile faded and her lashes swept up to see

that the color of his eyes had darkened and a flame had begun to flicker in their depths. Slowly she shook her head.

"That's too bad," he murmured, and lowered his head.

He outlined her mouth with kisses, taking extraordinary care not to touch her lips, then he turned his attention to her jawline, then her neck. He had been supporting his weight with a hand on either side of her, but gradually he lowered his body onto hers.

A compelling tension began to pulse in her, a different kind of trouble developed with her breathing, a beautiful, unbearable desire unfolded in her.

He changed position frequently to give himself a better angle for his kisses. Sometimes he shifted only an inch to the left, sometimes it was several inches to the right, other times it was up or down. But each movement caused her chiffon skirt to wrinkle, fold over on itself, inch down, inch up. The material rubbed against her, sensitizing her skin, heating her thighs. And as his chest slid this way and that over her, her breasts swelled and started to ache.

He skimmed his mouth down to where her breasts mounded above the low neckline of the beaded bodice. "I can feel your heart pounding," he whispered. "Are you ready to say you're sorry and accept me as a qualified challenger?"

He lifted the neckline of the bodice and licked beneath its edge to a taut nipple. She jerked at the thrill of desire that knifed into her. Then in a movement so fast she didn't realize what he had done until it was over, he reached behind her, unzipped the dress, and pulled the front down until he could get his whole mouth over the nipple.

The pleasure was excruciatingly intense, and she cried out. Threading her fingers into his hair, she pushed her head back against a cushion. Unable to control the need building in her, she went with it, giving herself up to the throbbing, the aching, the passion. She arched her hips up to his and felt a hardness that sent electricity sparking through her.

His mouth came down on hers, and his hand delved beneath the layers of chiffon to the silky smoothness of her legs. His tongue tangled with hers, his mind hazed over. Raw need gripped his body. He hadn't meant their tennis game to end like this. He certainly hadn't brought her to the court to make love to her. Had he? No.

He had vowed not to rush her. And he wouldn't. He *had* to cease this madness soon. And he would. . . .

His fingers thrust between her thighs to her warmth and softness.

Inflamed, she twisted violently beneath him, then her hips began to move in rhythm to his caresses. It was wonderful, but she'd been empty for so long. She craved his maleness, his power. She pulled on his hair until he lifted his head and gazed down at her.

"Do you want me to stop?" he asked thickly, unable to mask either his desire or his confusion. Then because he hoped it might put him back in the game-playing mood, he added, "Are you ready to say you're sorry?" It didn't work. He was burning for her.

"No, but I'm ready to say I want you. I *want* you, Conall. More than I can say, more than I can bear. Make love to me."

A hard shudder convulsed his body. "We'll go back to the suite."

"No! Here! Now!" She arched up to him again. "Oh, please, Conall."

The urgency and naked need in her voice galvanized him. Pushed nearly beyond endurance, he yanked her panties free of her legs and entered her with a force that fused them together. Ecstasy closed around Conall, narrowing his world to Sharon and the overwhelming intensity of the sensations that crashed through him again and again. Her legs fastened around him; his hips lifted and fell in a hard, fast rhythm.

He was no longer thinking. Something dark and primal had taken over, driving him. He was half mad, wanting her, needing her, *having* her. He thrust deeper into her, and suddenly they were straining together as her climax started, then his. He groaned, she cried out. It continued on and on, seeming to grow more powerful, more rapturous, until at last he emptied into her. And she was filled.

Sharon shifted. Her bare legs slid across silk and encountered something immovable. Slowly she opened her eyes. *Conall.* His face was only inches from hers.

She remembered now. They had waited for the trembling of their muscles to abate, then somehow dressed and walked back to the house, arm in arm. And when they had reached the suite, she had gone with him to his bedroom, where they had made love again just as frantically and just as hungrily as they had at the tennis court.

She lifted her head and gazed around the room. Her turquoise gown lay in a frothy pool on the floor next to his dark evening clothes. She lowered her head gently back to the pillow so as not to wake him, and she stared at the ceiling, experiencing a feeling of absolute surprise.

She was lying in the massive sleigh bed with him beneath the royal purple spread.

They had actually made love.

And it had been the greatest, most joyous experience she had ever had.

And not once during that time had she thought about trying to get pregnant.

Instead, she had been consumed by him, what he was doing to her, what she was doing to him, and how they were making each other feel.

Making love on a couch in an indoor tennis court where the light was pearlized and a stained glass roof curved above them hadn't been in her plans. She had envisioned a perfunctory act of sex, followed by twenty minutes of her lying with her bottom elevated on a pillow. Making love a second time so soon after the first time hadn't been in the program either. Every other day was best, she had read, to give the sperm a chance to build up and then be released in larger numbers. She seemed to remember that hot baths were out for the man, too, and Conall had had one right before dinner. Oh, well, they would just have to do better next time. They would wait a day, be more practical about their surroundings.

For some inexplicable reason she giggled and turned her head along the pillow to look at Conall.

His eyes were open. "I really like the way you laugh," he murmured huskily.

"I suppose laughing *is* a major talent."

"You mean sort of like your talent to win at tennis?" He slipped his arm beneath her back and pulled her up and over until she lay on top of him.

Her hair tumbled forward, and the soft golden-brown curls brushed against his chest and face.

She tucked one side behind her ear so that she could see him better. "What can I say? I'm just a very talented person."

"I would have to agree with that." He raised his head to kiss her lightly, briefly. "Although," he continued when his head was once again on the pillow, "our discussion regarding a rematch is not over."

"I'll look forward to our next talk on the subject," she said solemnly. "Almost as much as I'm looking forward to breakfast."

"You're hungry?"

"Starved."

"Funny, I am too. Why don't we order room service? What would you like?"

She chewed on her bottom lip a moment, thinking. "Do you have any idea what kind of champagne they have here? For instance, do you think they'd have something really old and rare?"

"There should be some Roederer Cristal 1945." He smoothed his hand down her bare back with absentminded possessiveness. "Would you like me to order it? Perhaps with some peaches?"

"Peaches?" She grinned. "Heavens no. I don't want to *drink* it. I want them to make us some champagne jelly from it. If they do it right away, we could have it for breakfast tomorrow."

He closed his eyes on a groan. "The wine steward is going to resign."

She used the pads of her thumbs to gently pry his lids up. "You don't think they'll do it?"

He blinked her thumbs away and glared at her. "I suppose you want to bet."

"I'm a businesswoman."

He sighed. "How much?"

"Four dollars. You've already given me two dollars for the raspberries. If we get the de-eyed black-eyed peas today for lunch, you'll owe me three dollars, and with the four dollars I'm sure to win for the jelly, that will be—"

He put his hand over her mouth. "Okay, on one condition. You place the order. Now, let's decide what we want for breakfast *this* morning."

She rolled off him and onto her back, then stretched, luxuriating in how comfortable and at ease she was with him. She had been briefly afraid that she might feel stiff and awkward with him after last night, but that was not the case at all. "Conall? Is that painting of the sea and the nude valuable?"

"Very."

"Oh." She paused. "Well, are you very attached to it?"

He came up on an elbow and gazed down at her. "Why? Are you going to ask the staff to decoupage it?"

She playfully swatted at his chest. "No. I was only wondering if we could replace it with a nice landscape. Something a little less . . . oppressively erotic."

"Do you have something against oppressively erotic?"

"On the whole, I'm very pro-erotic. It's the oppressive part that I'm not certain of."

"Say no more. I'll have Winston switch the painting."

"Thank you. Now, there's one more thing."

He groaned. "Is this going to be another bet? Because if it is, you should know that I've just about committed the extent of my cash reserves to you."

She skimmed a finger back and forth over his bottom lip. "No, it's not another bet. But in the future and as a personal favor to you, I will try to keep your financial crisis in mind. However, for now, do you think we could skip breakfast? I'd much rather make love."

"You know, Sharon, you're a little strange, but you're growing on me." He gathered her close and he bent to kiss her.

Seven

Leather creaked as Sharon turned in the saddle to glance back the way she and Conall had just ridden. She hadn't been able to see the house for quite some time and couldn't judge how far they had come. "Are we still on SwanSea land?"

"Definitely," Conall said, riding beside her.

"When are you going to tell me where we're going? Or why we're going there?"

"When we get there."

"There *where*? Conall Deverell, you're driving me crazy."

He looked across at her and grinned. "What's the problem? You liked last night's surprise, didn't you? The tennis court?"

In another life she would have blushed at the intimate look he sent her. Now she smiled. "Of course I remember."

His grin broadened. "Yeah, well, I remember too. And I guarantee that you're going to like this place. Besides, what difference does it make where I'm taking you? You're not in Boston. You're not on a timetable. There's nothing you have to do, nowhere you have to be. Relax."

She was relaxed, she thought, and at the

moment, almost indecently content. On her right, white-tipped waves rolled, one after the other, into the shore. To her left, purple and white asters, sky-blue gentians, and cardinal flowers grew wild in green meadows. Beyond the meadows, sugar maples displayed outrageously brilliant colors of red, orange, and gold. With nature's beauty to gaze at and Conall by her side, how could she complain?

"We're going to take the path up ahead and ride down to the beach," he said, breaking into her thoughts. "Pull in behind me and follow. It's an easy descent. Just go slow."

She nodded, doing as he said, and soon found herself guiding her horse onto the sand.

The tide had gone out, leaving a wide stretch of beach on which they could ride. Gulls swooped and dived, then chose a wind current, banked, and flew back out to sea. The sun coiled through the weave of her sweater to warm her skin. The breeze tossed more curl into her hair.

She laughed with delight. "It's been years since I've been on a beach. This is wonderful."

A wide smile split his face. "Winter, summer, spring, or fall, if I'm at SwanSea, I have to come down here. There's nothing like the enormity, the energy, the vast sweep of the ocean to put things into perspective for me."

She could understand his need for the solitude of the beach. She had seen for herself how weary he had been that first night he had arrived. The weight of responsibility on his shoulders was enormous. Uniquely qualified and able to carry that load of responsibility, he also needed times of rest and comfort.

They rode a short distance, then with a glance over his shoulder to make sure she was with him, he reined his horse around an outjutting of the cliff and onto a deep but shorter stretch of beach.

When she followed, she saw a shallow recess hollowed into the side of the cliff and, spread there, a large blanket with wicker baskets sitting on it.

"A picnic?" she asked, amazed. "How did you manage it?"

He eased back on the reins, pulled his horse to a stop, and dismounted. "*You're* asking that? You with your undying faith in the staff?"

She rolled her eyes. "You're right. I don't know how to explain it, except I obviously lost my mind there for a minute. I'm sure we even have a container of de-eyed black-eyed peas over there. What do you want to bet?"

"Three dollars. How could you forget?" He held up his arms for her and swung her to the ground.

Hand in hand they crossed the sand together. She dropped down onto the big, soft blanket and began to unpack one of the wicker baskets. Not too far away, driftwood was neatly stacked for a fire. Conall knelt to light it and waited a minute to make sure it had caught.

"We have china, we have silver, we have crystal, we have linen napkins," she said as he walked back to her, then continued to recite everything she had found in the wicker baskets. She finished with, "And last but not least, we have a container of something steaming hot that looks like taupe-colored library paste."

He peered into the container. "The black-eyed peas?"

She nodded. "*Sans* black eyes. You know, I'm beginning to feel guilty. I don't think I can make any more of these requests of the staff."

"Oh, come on. They're enjoying it. *They* are making bets on what you'll ask for next. You're the only person who's ever given them any kind of real challenge."

"No, no, I just can't. They're all so sweet and willing to please. And by the way, you owe me three dollars."

"Hey! How about giving me some slack. You've never met anyone sweeter or more willing to please than me."

"Three dollars, Conall."

"But what about the critical condition of my cash reserves?"

"Three dollars, Conall."

Glaring at her, he dug into his jeans for his wallet, pulled out three dollars, and handed them to her. Then he leapt on her, knocking her over backward, and smacked kisses all over her face and throat while he tickled her. Tears of laughter were running down her cheeks, and she was gasping for breath when he finally stopped. He sat up and pulled her upright beside him.

She wiped the tears of mirth from her cheeks and fixed him with an equally glaring stare. "You really are a sore loser, aren't you?"

He shrugged. "I've always had a difficult time dealing with the concept of losing."

"You know something else about you?" she asked, pointing a finger at him with narrowed eyes. "It's very interesting the way you use kisses as punishment. I feel strongly that it all stems from your warped childhood."

"Warped? Excuse me?"

"You were never punished, so you don't know what real punishment is. Poor kid." She glanced at the banquet spread out before them. "Are we hungry yet?"

He laughed and pressed a kiss to her cheek. "Yes, I think we are, especially since we seem to have missed breakfast."

They ate in companionable silence. Afterward, they took a long walk. When they returned, Conall added wood to the fire, and they dropped back down onto the blanket.

"I really like this place," she murmured, drawing her knees up to her chest and gazing out at the sea. "It has a cozy, secluded feeling to it. Thank you for bringing me here. And thank you also for the picnic. It was very thoughtful of you."

Listening to her, he realized that despite the softness of her voice there was a formality to what she was saying. It was as if she were a guest thanking her host. The idea made him angry, and he tried to understand why.

He *was* playing the part of host, he supposed, but under the circumstances, surely it seemed normal. After all, he knew SwanSea and she didn't. He could show her things she wouldn't otherwise know existed. Still, the normal roles of guest and host implied a certain distance between them. Could that be why he was angry?

"You know," Sharon said reflectively, "family lore has it that my great-aunt Clarisse never visited SwanSea. I wish she could have."

"Do you know why she didn't?"

"Apparently she had the opportunity and turned it down. Her relationship with Jake pretty much ended when he graduated from Harvard. Her choice, not his." Her mouth twisted, and her eyes took on a faraway look. "I remember my father yelling at me how inconceivable it was to him that two women from the same family could have *both* bungled landing a Deverell man." Her bark of laughter expressed anything but amusement.

Conall's expression hardened. "I don't want to upset you, Sharon, but I think what your father did was despicable. Turning your back on your

own child at a time when they desperately need
you is beyond my comprehension. If he wasn't
dead, I think I would kill him myself."

"Don't say that."

"I'm sorry, but—"

"He was my father, Conall, no matter what he
did."

"That's right, and you were his daughter, dammit. You shouldn't have had to go through what
you did alone."

His vehemence surprised her. "It's over."

"Maybe, but you still seem pretty much alone
to me."

"I can take care of myself."

He turned to her, obviously troubled. "I know
the baby wasn't mine, but shortly after I beat the
hell out of Mark, someone told me that he left the
country. I—" He broke off.

"Yes?" she prompted, uncertain what he was
trying to say.

"I knew nothing about the situation with your
parents, but knowing that the baby's father was
gone as I did, I should have checked on you to
make sure you had everything you needed. It
would have been the decent thing to do."

She shook her head. "There was too much
anger and pain between us for either of us to try
and do the 'decent' thing."

He took her arms in a hard grip, his eyes
glittering.

"But don't you see? I should have done more
for you. If I had, maybe you wouldn't have lost
your baby."

She raised her hand and curved her palm along
his jaw. "No, Conall. The doctor said it was no
one's fault. Nothing I did or didn't do. Nothing
anyone did or didn't do." Sadness entered her
voice. "He said when a woman miscarries that

early in a pregnancy, there is usually a good reason, and that I shouldn't allow myself to agonize over it."

"And were you able to take his advice?"

"As time went on, it got easier."

"Dear God, but I wish things could have been different!"

She was stunned. Never in a million years would she have imagined that they would be having this conversation. Never in a million years would she have imagined that *she* would be trying to comfort him.

"Don't dwell on it, Conall. I don't."

"Don't you?"

She shook her head. "No. I went forward and built a new, shinier life."

His brow furrowed, as if he were trying to understand something. "But you're here with me now. Isn't that, in a way, going backward?"

She'd wondered the same thing more than once. "If that's what I'm doing, it's only for a very short while and for a definite purpose."

Irritation crept along his nerves, but he pushed his annoyance away in favor of asking her something he'd been wondering about for some time. "Do you think what we felt for each other back then was really love?"

This question was easier for her to answer. "Absolutely. Just because it was a first love didn't make it any less love. There's nothing more intense and wondrous than a first love. We were caught up in a whirl of excitement and expectation. The whole world looked different back then."

His lips curved softly as he thought about what she'd said. "It did, didn't it?"

Old resentments were fading. Old pain was breaking apart and dissolving. And she wasn't sure if that was good. "It was a time that will never come again," she said firmly. "Nor should it."

A helplessness swelled up inside Conall, but he told himself he had to be mistaken about the emotion he was feeling. The only time he had ever truly felt helpless was when the doctor had told him he would never be a father. He'd figure it all out later—the irritation, the helplessness. Right now he had the greatest urge to make love to her.

"Maybe you're right. Maybe we should just concentrate on the present." He took her hand and brought the palm to his mouth. "Did you know there's a sweetness to your skin," he murmured, "and a perfume?"

Her heart jerked against her rib cage. "Is there?"

"Yes, and you know what else? I think we went too fast last night."

"Do you?"

"All three times," he said huskily. "This time I want to go slowly. I want to reacquaint myself with your body, relearn you until I know you blind. Then I want to learn new things about you that I never knew before."

He lowered her gently onto the blanket and stretched out beside her, his body touching hers. Propping himself up with his elbow, he slipped his hand beneath her sweater and rested it on the firm flesh just below her breasts.

"The inferno we were caught up in last night is out," he said huskily. "Now let's rebuild it, degree by degree."

On the surface he appeared completely controlled. His face showed composure, his voice sounded calm, his hand rested lightly on her. But in the depths of his eyes there was a burning so fierce, she felt it all the way to her toes.

"That sounds like a wonderful idea," she murmured. She pulled her sweater up her body, rose slightly, brought it over her head, and tossed it aside. Her bra followed. She lay back down; holding his eyes, watching their color deepen with his every heartbeat and her every movement, she reached down and stripped off her shoes and socks, then unbuttoned her jeans and peeled them off. Finally all that was left was her panties.

In moments she was completely naked.

He sucked in a hard breath. "And here I thought I wanted to undress you slowly. You knew better than I did what I really wanted. You amaze me."

A wave rolled into shore, and several more; then he lay beside her as bare as she.

He threaded his fingers through hers and raised their joined hands until they rested on the blanket behind her head.

"Last night you told me you wanted me," he said, his voice thickening with every word. "Tell me again."

"I want you," she whispered.

"Tell me again," he muttered.

"I want you, Conall," she said softly, as if she were stroking him with her voice. "Now you tell me."

"Dear God, don't you know, can't you see?" His hand rubbed compulsively over her, from below her breasts to down past her navel, then back again. "I'm in pain, I want you so much. But I'm still determined we're going to take this slowly. We have all the time in the world. Last night we were starved for each other. Now we've fed." He bent his head to her breast.

She'd never been in such an erotic situation, she thought hazily, a heated quivering beginning in her. Even the otherworldly tennis court couldn't match this setting. A cashmere blanket over smooth golden sand. A glorious blue sky dotted by soft white clouds. A cool autumn breeze, a hot driftwood fire. The strength of the ocean. The grace of the sea birds.

Here there was nothing to confine them, no half-shed clothes to hinder their eagerness, no couch to restrict their zeal and energy. No walls to enclose their passion. No glass roof to muffle their cries.

He slid inside her, suddenly and so easily it was almost as if he hadn't withdrawn from her last night or this morning. It was as if he were a permanent part of her.

Slowly he began to rock inside her. She had intended to do as he had said and set a leisurely pace, to savor him and this lovemaking to the ultimate, like a miser with his gold, like an art student in the Sistine Chapel, like a lover of all that is beautiful standing on the north rim of the Grand Canyon at sunset.

But the pleasure didn't come leisurely. At his first gentle thrust it tore through her and threatened to rip her apart. She gasped, then moaned, and he covered her mouth with his.

"I love the sounds you make when I'm inside you," he murmured raggedly, his breathing rough but his strokes even and steady. "I'd like to make a tape of them. I'd play them over and over." Agony racked his body; sweat glistened on his skin. Like fire burning through a forest, his ever-increasing passion was eating its way through his discipline and restraint at raging speed. "But if I taped those sounds—ahhh!—I could never be apart from you, because I'd stay in a perpetual state of heat for you. Pretty much as I've been since you came back into my life."

A whimper escaped from her as she writhed beneath him.

"There, like that! If I heard that and you weren't with me, I'd tear down buildings to get to you." He was pushing himself beyond his endurance, but somehow, he told himself, he had to hold on. He wanted this to last and last and last.

Her lower body was engorged with a feverish need. Her sanity hung by threads. Urgently, she arched up to him, but nothing she did seemed to change his tempo. He continued to move in and out of her with sleek animal grace and measured strength.

"You're driving me mad," she said, and wrapped her legs around his waist.

He ground his teeth together until he felt pain. "Dammit, we should be able to make it last!"

"Next time," she said, raising her head to press her mouth to his ear, ready to promise him anything. "Next time we will." Her voice choked. "Lord, Conall—"

He let himself go and pumped into her with all his might.

She reveled in his ruthless hunger and all-encompassing need. It matched hers.

He was power, he was passion.

And at that moment he was hers.

Day followed day, and Sharon reveled in each one. The idyllic times she and Conall were sharing were beyond her imagination. In some ways they seemed more like a dream than reality.

If occasionally she heard a soft warning voice in her head, she ignored it. And anyway, there was never any time to listen. She was too busy playing with Conall, swimming, riding, frolicking on the beach, engaging in midnight tennis matches.

And then there was the lovemaking. Every time they came together, it was more incredible.

She had been at SwanSea just over a week when the voice in her head began to grow louder, more insistent.

You're in love with him, the voice said.

Of course I'm not, she replied.

You're in love with him.

No, no, no. It's natural that I respond to him. He's a very accomplished lover. But I'm not in love with him.

You're in love with him.

No— Her heart seemed to stop beating for a moment. Dear Lord, she was hopelessly, completely, irrevocably in love with Conall.

And then she knew what had been worrying her about her plan. She had completely overlooked this mind-blowing possibility.

She had fallen in love with him despite the fact that he still did not believe the child she had conceived ten years earlier was his. She had tried to prepare so carefully for these two weeks with him. Mentally, she had believed she could handle their time together with cool detachment, and then when the time was up, leave him without so much as sustaining a single bruise or a hurt.

Somewhere along the way she had lost control of the situation. And, she acknowledged with sorrow, her loss of control might be traced to the day she had presented Jake's note to Conall at his office.

This love for him seemed to have come out of nowhere. But had it really? Maybe that love had been in her all along. It had occurred to her that unconsciously she might have had another reason to ask him to father her child. Now she knew the real truth was she didn't just want the child, she wanted Conall too.

Maybe she wanted him most of all.

You're not following any of the procedures that would make getting pregnant easier, she whispered to herself.

It was true. She forgot for long stretches of time the reason she had come to SwanSea, and when she and Conall made love, getting pregnant was the last thing on her mind.

It won't matter, she told the voice in her head. I became pregnant the first time without all the careful planning. I'll do it again.

But what if you don't?

What?

What if you don't become pregnant?

Her breath caught in her throat and ice slid down her spine. Oh, dear heaven. If she didn't become pregnant, she would never be able to convince Conall that she hadn't betrayed him by sleeping with Mark.

Conall insisted that they be together all the time; it was obvious he enjoyed being with her. And the intensity of his lovemaking showed more than words that he desired her. Lifetime relationships had been built on less than these two things. But if by chance they could work out some kind of future together, he would never be able to trust her. Not if she couldn't get pregnant.

The doctor had told him he had a very small chance of fathering a child, yet they had conceived a child together. Looking back on it, she realized her pregnancy had been something of a miracle. But when you were eighteen, scared, and all alone, miracles were not on your mind. Apparently ten years hadn't changed anything.

Dear heavens, why hadn't she realized before now what a ridiculously long shot it was for her to become pregnant?

Because you love him, have always loved him.

Yes, she replied.

A storm raged around the great house of SwanSea the next night. Rain slashed at the stone walls, lightning bright as day lit the rooms, thunder crashed as if the sky and SwanSea's heart was breaking apart.

It was as if the house knew what she was about to do and didn't approve, Sharon thought, lying beside Conall in his bed.

No, she couldn't think about it. The arrangements were made, and she had no intention of backing out. She had to leave.

Her bags were packed and in the other bedroom. A cab would be waiting at the bottom of the drive for her. A small chartered plane was gassed and ready at the airport. It was two-thirty now. She would leave in thirty minutes.

She listened to Conall's even breathing and said a small, silent prayer of thanks that he was sleeping so soundly. He had no idea that she planned to bolt, and she didn't have the heart or the mental strength to tell him. Their two weeks wouldn't be up for another four days. He would argue with her; more than likely she would give in. And that wouldn't be good for either of them.

No, it was best she leave. No matter which way she looked at their situation, she saw impossibility. He would never trust her, and without trust there was no love. And if by some chance she did become pregnant, was in fact already pregnant—

No, it was best she leave. She would never be able to believe he wanted her for her sake alone if she were pregnant.

Besides, she had other plans, plans she had made right from the beginning.

Carefully, so as not to disturb him, she rose up on her elbow and softly kissed him. Then she slipped from the bed and went into the other room. She dressed quickly, and carrying her luggage, left the house by a back door.

The storm was moving out to sea. The time between the claps of thunder and bursts of lightning was longer now. And the rain had slackened.

But SwanSea remained as always: A sentry standing guard, protector of its own.

As the cab started away, Sharon turned in the seat to rub the condensation from the rear window. She wanted to get one last glimpse of the place where for a short time she had known such happiness.

What she saw didn't surprise her.

Black clouds scudded over the chimney tops of the great house. Around it, trees bowed with the wind. No light shone from its windows.

SwanSea was fiercely angry.

Sharon was gone.

At first, when Conall awoke to find her missing from the bed, he assumed she had gotten up early and gone downstairs to breakfast or for a ride. But since she had never done either of those things without him, he soon began to look for her. And when he couldn't find her in any of the obvious places, he turned to the staff.

They had made champagne jelly for him from a rare and expensive vintage of wine, and they had divided M&M's by color for him, but they couldn't find Sharon for him.

She was gone.

Eight

Conall flung a file folder down on his desk and shot a killing look at his phone. He'd been back in Boston just over twenty-four hours, and during that time there hadn't been too many minutes when his mind hadn't been on Sharon and whether or not he should call her.

His emotions were in turmoil. He didn't understand why she had left, but he especially didn't understand how she could have bolted without telling him or even giving any indication of what she planned to do.

He had never laughed as much with anyone as he had with her. He had never known such ecstasy. He had enjoyed their quiet times together just as much as he had those times when they were being outrageous. And he would have bet everything he owned that she felt the same way.

He was hurt, and he was hurting.

Dammit, why hadn't she called him since her return?

Granted, he hadn't called her, but then he wasn't the one who had stolen out of SwanSea in the dead of night.

His hand went to the phone, then jerked away.

He knew why he hadn't called her. *Pride.* He had once heard his mother call pride the Achilles' heel of the Deverell men. A lot she knew.

He snatched up the receiver and punched out the number he had memorized over the last hours. It rang once, twice, and then was picked up.

"Hello, Sharon—"

He heard four very irritating tones, then a woman's voice. "We're sorry you have reached a number that has been disconnected or is no longer in service. If you feel you have reached this recording in error, please check the number or try your call again. This is a recording."

He slammed the receiver back in its cradle. *Disconnected?* What in the hell kind of game was Sharon playing? When he got hold of her, he was going to wring her lovely neck—

He tensed. What if she had been hurt? What if she were sick? Lord, what if she were in some kind of danger? He hadn't seen or spoken to her since sometime after midnight two nights before. *Anything* could have happened to her.

His heart racing madly, he shot out of his chair and dashed for the door.

Boston traffic had never seemed worse, and by the time he arrived at the brownstone where she lived, his nerves felt like live electrical wires, arching and sparking high voltage.

He bounded up the stairs, ready to tear into her for worrying him so, for leaving him.

He pounded on the door with his fist. "Sharon? Come on, answer the door, dammit."

A door downstairs opened and an old man appeared at the bottom of the stairs. "Here now, what's all the ruckus?"

Conall ignored the man and beat on the door again.

The man took hold of the handrail and with labored steps climbed the stairs. "Young man," he said when he reached Conall, "you're creating a helluva disturbance, plus you're wasting your time. Do us all a favor and stop before I have to call the police."

Conall rounded on him. "Do you know where Sharon Graham is?"

"No, but I do know she's not in that apartment. She moved out."

Conall went still. "That's impossible. She's been with me the last week or so and back here just a little over twenty-four hours. No one could move an entire apartment that quickly."

The man rocked back on his heels. "It would have been hard, all right, for her to do it that way. Not saying she couldn't have, you understand, but she didn't. She had everything boxed and ready to go when she left town. Then while she was gone, some movers came in, packed it up in a truck, and took off."

Conall's mind closed down, refusing to accept what he was hearing. "Who has the key to this apartment? I want to see for myself."

The man eyed Conall warily, but pulled a set of keys from his pockets. "I'm the landlord, and I'll be glad to let you have a look, but you'll have to promise not to do any damage." At Conall's terse nod, he inserted the key and opened the door for him.

"Will you be long?"

"I don't know."

"Well, just knock on my door on your way out so that I'll know you've left."

Conall had half expected her to be there, as if this were all some weird joke she was playing on him and he hadn't gotten the punch line. But he found, instead, an emptiness so complete it staggered him.

The walls, the windows, the floors, *everything* was bare. The apartment had been stripped. All her fragrance, all signs of her personality had vanished . . . as if she had never even been in those rooms, much less lived there.

His footsteps echoed hollowly as he walked down the short hall. In the kitchen he opened and closed a few cabinets but found nothing. A phone sat on the counter beside a dog-eared Boston phone book. He knew the phone had been disconnected but picked it up anyway. The line was dead.

An awful desolation swamped him.

He walked back into the living room, remembering the first night he had come to the apartment. He had been bothered by its femininity and charm. Looking back, he could see now that she had created a nest, a soft retreat from a hard world, a place to be nurtured and to nurture.

She had wanted a baby and had never tried to pretend any differently. Without wrapping the matter in pretty paper, she had told him straight out she wanted to use him to get her pregnant.

He wasn't sure from where her firm belief came that he could father a child for her. Perhaps because of the hell she'd gone through ten years before, her mind had *wished* so often that he was fertile, it had become true to her. Who knew what went on in another person's mind? He obviously didn't. Not hers, at any rate.

Maybe she had left because she had finally accepted he was unable to give her the child she wanted. Maybe, wherever she'd moved, she'd find someone who could make her pregnant and she'd finally have the happiness she deserved.

He closed his eyes as a wave of pain hit him.

Let her go in peace, Conall, he told himself. *She's had enough torment in her life. Let her go.*

"Did she give the landlord a forwarding address?" Amarillo asked, scribbling in a small brown leather notebook.

Conall shook his head, his expression bleak.

"All right, but I'll check back with him anyway. I want to see the apartment myself."

"There's nothing there." Conall stared sightlessly at his desk. "It's totally empty. She didn't leave so much as a scrap of paper behind. But you should have seen it when she lived there. It was warm, sweet, very homey."

Amarillo's tawny-gold eyes narrowed on him. "Don't worry about the forwarding address. I can check with the phone and utility companies. She will have given them an address where they can send the closing bills. Then there's her bank. If she's left town, she will sooner or later transfer her money to a bank near her new place of residence. In this society, there's a hell of a lot of paperwork, and paper leaves a trail."

Conall plucked a sleek gold ball-point pen from its black marble-based holder, studied it as if he weren't sure why it was in his hand, then returned the pen to its sheath. "It's hard for me to believe that she set these plans in motion before we even went to SwanSea. All that time we were together there, she knew she was going to do this."

Amarillo studied the tip of one boot. "Are you sure you want me to find her?"

Conall blinked, his mental haze cleared, and the sandy-haired man sitting across from him came into sharp, clear focus. "I'm absolutely sure."

"Think about it. Maybe it would be best to drop it."

"I can't."

"Are you sure? What she's done is stone cold calculating, not to mention devious as hell."

"Or maybe it's desperate. No, Rill, I want her found, and I want her found as soon as possible."

Amarillo expelled a long breath, then checked his notebook. "Okay, then. We'll do it your way. Is there anything else you can think of that I should know? Names of friends? Clubs or organizations to which she might have belonged?"

"Did I tell you where she works?" He grimaced. "Worked, I mean."

Amarillo nodded.

"Then, that's all I know. Hell, I can't even tell you if she owns a car or not."

Amarillo closed his notebook, leaned back in the chair, and looked at his friend with a gaze that held an innate wisdom and a wealth of experience, not all of it good. "You know, don't you, that you're in love with her?"

"I know," Conall said quietly. "I know."

"You look like hell," Amarillo said, dropping down into a chair in Conall's den and grimly surveying the three-day growth of beard on his face.

"Thanks."

"Have you slept, or is that a foolish question? And how about food?"

"Forget food, forget sleep. How about Sharon? Have you found her?"

"The lady doesn't want to be found, Conall. It's as simple as that."

"Are you trying to tell me you can't find her?"

The gold eyes glittered. "I'll never tell you that because I don't give up. Ever. I will find her. But it's going to take time, maybe a lot of time."

Conall wearily rubbed his face. "What have you learned?"

"To begin with, I can tell you with complete assurance that no one has left this city in the last week by plane, train, or bus with a ticket in the name of Sharon Graham. Her landlord told me that as long as she lived at the brownstone—which was four years, by the way—she didn't own a car, and I can find no recent records that she's bought one. That means she's either still in Boston, or she flew out of here using another name."

"She's not here in Boston." Conall's tone was flat.

"How do you know?"

He shrugged. "It's just a feeling. Boston seems so . . . so empty."

"Uh-huh. Well, you may be right. Oh, another thing. She's withdrawn all her money from her bank, and let me tell you, it was quite a large sum."

Conall frowned. "Withdrawn. In what form?"

"Cash. All in twenties. All untraceable. She carried it out in a large case over the *strong* objections of the bank officers."

Conall shot up out of his chair. "Damn. What were they thinking of to let her walk out of there with all that money? That's dangerous!"

"It was her money. They couldn't stop her."

"You say it was a lot of money?"

Amarillo nodded. "Her salary was quite good, and she lived modestly, obviously saving most of it. Plus, you said her mother had died last year. I'm sure there was an inheritance."

"Yes," he said, thinking of Jake's note containing the promise he had made to Clarisse. Jake's promise had played havoc with his grandson's emotional life. Yet without that note, Sharon would never have come back to him.

"With the amount of money she was able to withdraw, she'll be able to live quite well. You've nothing to worry about on that score. The problem is, cash dealings leave no record. That's how she paid off the utility companies. Therefore, there's no forwarding address." A look of pain creased Conall's face, and Amarillo expelled a long breath. "Now, about the movers who loaded up her boxes and furniture while you were at SwanSea. Once again she was very careful. According to the landlord, they were young men and they drove a truck with no company name on it, no writing whatsoever. And I've checked with all the moving companies. Nothing."

"Dammit, Rill, they can't *all* be dead ends."

"Everyone makes mistakes. It just may take a while for Sharon to make one. Be patient."

Conall closed his eyes. "You have no idea what you're asking."

Watching him, Amarillo thought he did. Conall looked as a man must who was trying to function with his heart torn out.

Six weeks after Sharon disappeared from SwanSea, Conall received an express letter from San Francisco marked personal. His secretary brought it into him unopened.

He broke the seal and pulled a single sheet of paper from the envelope. It was a medical report from a doctor dated five days before. It stated that Sharon Clarisse Graham was approximately seven weeks pregnant.

The words blurred, the report slipped from his fingers.

Dear God in heaven, she'd been right all along.

He'd made her pregnant ten years ago. And now, once again, she carried his child, once again all alone.

He reached for his phone. "Find Amarillo and tell him I want to see him immediately."

An hour later, when Amarillo walked into the office, Conall was staring out the window, the medical report in his hand.

"What's up?"

Conall swung his chair around and handed him the report.

Amarillo scanned the report. "This may be the break we've been waiting for."

"I was hoping you'd say that. Do you think you can find out anything from the doctor?"

"I'm not sure if there'll be that much to find out from him. This is only a test, Conall. She may have been in San Francisco just long enough to have this test taken, then moved on." Distress crossed Conall's face. "Don't worry," Amarillo said. "I will do everything in my power to find out something. But in the event I'm right and she's moved on . . ."

"Yes?"

"Sharon left one thing behind when she left. A local phone book."

"I know, I saw it, but—"

"People sometimes circle numbers in their phone books. Sometimes they even write numbers in it, especially emergency numbers. I took the phone book home with me. She wrote a doctor's number on the inside cover; I assume it's her family doctor. Now, pregnant women need prenatal care, and whoever gives it to them usually requests that their previous doctors send them their records, especially, I would imagine, if there'd been another pregnancy that had ended short of term. I think it will be worthwhile for me to monitor her doctor."

"Monitor?"

Amarillo grinned. "Trade secrets."

"Do whatever you have to do. In the meantime, I'm going to make a doctor's appointment myself."

Four months later Conall stood on a sidewalk in a quiet neighborhood in San Diego, California, and gazed at a small bungalow across the street.

A stained glass hummingbird hung in the front window. A ceramic rabbit played among the geraniums in the flower bed.

At last, he had found her.

He crossed the street, walked up the sidewalk, and knocked. Several nerve-racking minutes passed. A car drove by on the street behind him. He heard hedge clippers being run several houses down. Finally the door opened and Sharon appeared on the threshold.

As soon as she saw who it was, her eyes widened with panic.

The flat of his palm hit the door just in time to stop her from slamming it in his face. "I've come all the way across the country to see you," he said quietly. "Aren't you going to invite me in?"

"No."

With one quick glimpse he took in the shadows beneath her eyes and the paleness of her skin. "I'm afraid I'm going to have to insist."

He gently pushed past her. Inside, he saw that she had duplicated her apartment in Boston, using the same furnishings and more important, the same loving care. He absorbed the familiar surroundings, then began to notice one or two new items. A porcelain calico cat had joined the English spaniel on the fireplace hearth. Another Hummel figurine had come to live among the stoneware children, this one a girl standing beside a baby buggy, her hands folded in prayer.

And lastly, there was a large box propped in a corner with a picture of a cradle on it.

She had created another nest.

Sharon self-consciously folded her arms over her swollen stomach, then realized that the slacks and oversize blouse she wore covered her well. And what did it matter anyway? "How did you find me?"

"It wasn't easy. You have the complete admiration of Amarillo Smith, something that not many people can boast about."

"I'm sure it's an honor."

Her sarcasm briefly lifted his brows. "How are you?"

"Fine."

"Why don't I believe you?"

"I haven't the faintest idea. Would you please leave now?"

"No," he said, and as if to emphasize his point, walked to the nearest chair and sat down.

Sharon steeled herself to cope with his presence. He was filling the small house to bursting. He pressed in on her without touching her, depleting her already-low reserves of strength.

This was a moment she'd hoped and prayed would never come. She'd worked so hard, gone to such lengths to insure that he would never find her. He would want an explanation, but there was none she could give him that could approach the truth—the truth being that she had fallen in love with him.

He propped his elbows on the chair's arms and

steepled his fingers. "Why did you leave SwanSea without telling me?"

"Haven't you figured it out yet? I left because I'm not a nice person. Did you have Winston Lawrence count the silver?"

He rubbed his temple thoughtfully. "Sit down, Sharon. You look like you're about to fall."

"I'm fine," she said again, but dropped down onto the couch.

His heart went out to her. She looked so defensive and so defenseless. He ached to hold her, to comfort her, but it seemed to him she'd crumple if he hit her with emotions that held any force at all. And he had to remember, she had every reason to hate him. "Okay, let's start again. Why didn't you tell me you planned to disappear?"

"Because I knew the moment you found out I was pregnant, you'd come looking for me and would want the baby. And if I didn't get pregnant, I didn't feel I wanted to go on living in the same area of the country as you." This had been the initial reason for her careful planning and move, but when she realized she loved him, her reasons had changed. After the intimacy they had shared at SwanSea, it would have been too painful to live so close to him, yet be so far away emotionally. It had been several weeks after she left SwanSea before the idea she might be pregnant had even occurred to her.

He closed his eyes until the hurt had washed through him. "But you sent me the medical report."

She looked away. "I felt you deserved to know that you can father a child."

Gazing steadily at her, he slowly sat forward and rested his arms on his knees. "Apologies don't mean a thing, but I have to give you one anyway. I'm sorry I didn't believe you, Sharon. I am so very sorry."

Her lips twisted with a brief smile of pain. "But you believe me now because you went straight to your doctor when you received the medical report. Am I right?"

"As soon as I read the doctor's report I believed you. I didn't need confirmation."

Her expression was plainly disbelieving. "Did you or did you not go to the doctor?"

"Yes, I did. But only to find out what the hell happened ten years ago to screw up those tests." He looked down at his hands. "It seems my sperm count has built back up over the years. Apparently it happens that way sometime."

"And what did you find out about the tests taken ten years ago?"

"They were accurate. When the doctor told me I had a very slim chance of fathering a child, it devastated me. I walked out of his office in a daze and never gave a thought to the fact that I did have any chance at all. My only excuse is that when you hear there's something like a ninety-five percent chance it's going to rain, you forget about the five percent chance it's not."

"Except, Conall, in this case the subject was a baby, not rain."

"If you believe nothing else, believe that I will never forgive myself. There's nothing I can do to make it up to you, Sharon. Nothing."

"You're wrong. You can leave."

He straightened with a sigh. "That's the one thing I can't do."

Sharon's heart jumped with fear. "You can't have this baby. You can't!"

He lifted his hand, wanting to touch her but not daring to. "Calm down. I don't want to take your baby from you. I wouldn't do that."

"I managed to lose myself for six months. Next time I'll do a better job."

"Sharon, stop it. You're upsetting yourself."

She took a deep, shuddering breath. He was right. She had to get herself under control. But these last few months it had been so hard to discipline her emotions. Her hormones were running wild. One moment she would be happy and excited, the next, she would be crying. But the emotion that bothered her the most was the unreasoning and profound fear. It came upon her at the most unexpected times, wrapping around her, sapping her of spirit and courage, immobilizing her.

"Listen to me," Conall was saying. "I won't take your baby away from you, and to prove it, I'll sign any kind of document you want me to."

She put a hand to her head. He was confusing her. And to make her feel even worse, his effortless power, vitality, and energy was the exact opposite of what she was feeling.

"Sharon, why are there shadows under your eyes? Why are you so damned pale?"

His sudden questions took her by surprise. "I've been having a little trouble sleeping, that's all."

"What does the doctor say?"

"Get more rest."

"And is it a problem for you to do that?"

"No, no problem. Conall, what is it exactly that you want from me?"

"Nothing except to take care of you."

She was beginning to understand. "You feel guilty."

"Yes." Let her believe what she wanted. "I left you alone once before. I won't this time."

"It sounds like atonement."

"Call it what you wish. I am going to see you

through the birth of this child whether you want me to or not. I'm going to be there for you."

She eyed him warily. As much as she loved him, she didn't know if she could trust him. She had needed him so desperately ten years before and he had turned his back on her. There was a danger that she might grow to depend on him during the next few months, and then when the time came he would have changed his mind and wouldn't be there.

She rose and walked to the mantel, giving herself a minute to decide what she should do. She'd gone to such lengths to get away from him, and the hardest part, the planning, the packing and the unpacking, was over.

She was settled. And she couldn't see moving again, at least not until the baby had been born. True, Conall knew where she was now. But his life, his family, and his business were clear across the country. What could he do? *Don't be stupid, Sharon. He can do anything he wants to do.*

"I want to take you back to Boston with me," he said. "You'll get the best medical care there."

"And afterward?"

He hesitated. Losing her again would just about destroy him. But her welfare and peace of mind would have to come first. "I'd like you to stay in Boston—"

"Because of the child?"

If he told her he loved her, she'd laugh at him and then she'd yell at him. She hated him and she had every reason. "Yes, because of the baby. But if you want to come back here after the baby is born, I can't stop you."

She made a scoffing sound. "You can't? I thought a Deverell could do anything."

He smiled sadly. "Well, now you know differently."

"No, I don't. Not really."

"Sharon, you shouldn't be alone at a time like this. And if I have to move here to make sure you aren't, then I will. But if you'll come back to Boston with me, we'll leave all your things in place here and I'll hire someone to keep a regular check on the place. That way, when or if you decide to return, you'll know it will be here waiting for you. Or if you'd rather, we'll pack up everything and put it in storage. But the first thing we're going to do is deposit your damned money in a bank. I can't imagine what you were thinking of—certainly not your safety."

"I was thinking of getting away from you."

He recoiled as if she'd struck him, and immediately she regretted what she'd said.

She went on. "Anyway, I've already deposited the money. I got fake identification in Tijuana."

"Oh, great," he said wearily. "You went to Tijuana by yourself."

She pursed her lips, understanding there was no argument she could give him regarding Tijuana he would buy. "Where would I stay in Boston?"

"My house."

She shook her head. "No, no . . ."

"I wouldn't bother you. I promise."

She could hardly believe it, but her resolve was weakening. Being alone didn't bother her; she was used to it. And she knew being a single parent would be hard, but in her mind she had accepted the additional responsibility of a baby long ago. She had even planned that after the baby was born she would do a limited amount of accounting, making her office in her home, and taking on individuals and small businesses as clients.

Now, though, she was having to deal with fear,

and she didn't know whether she was strong enough to do so alone. Reluctant as she was to admit it, even to herself, his promise to be with her at the time of the baby's birth reassured her.

Her last visit to the doctor had taught her that no matter how hard you try, you cannot figure *everything* out on paper. He had told her that because of a narrow pelvis, she might have trouble delivering the baby and they might have to perform a cesarean section.

She'd been in a hospital as a patient only once, and it was that memory, plus its attendant nightmares, that had been keeping her awake nights.

She vividly recalled the blood, the pain, the gut-wrenching feeling that there was no one in the world who cared if she lived or died. And now, no matter how hard she tried, she couldn't make her fear of going back into a hospital vanish.

"You won't try to take my baby from me?" she asked, her voice shaky.

"I promise you that I won't."

"And afterward I can go anywhere I choose?"

"As soon as the doctor says you and the baby are in good shape."

Which would be worse, she wondered, living with the man she loved, knowing he didn't love her, and bearing his child with him by her side, knowing they would never be a family. Or facing alone her memories of that nightmare experience and the unknown of the reality.

Nine

Three months later, Sharon still didn't have an answer to her question.

Conall's home was luxurious, spacious, and decorated with discriminating, exquisite taste. He had given her a suite down the hall from his. Over the months, she had added her own touches to the elegantly furnished rooms. Several newly purchased Hummel children graced the mantel. A stained glass bluebird hung in one of the windows. Pink and blue yarn filled a wicker basket. Lately the blue yarn had started to dominate. And in her bedroom, the cradle she had bought in San Diego had been assembled and stood waiting.

Though she was living in Conall's house, she rarely saw him for any length of time. He left early in the morning and came home late at night.

But he made it a point to talk to her every day, either in person or by phone from his office. He always asked the same questions: How was she? Did she need anything? She always gave him the same reply. She was fine, and no, she didn't need a thing.

Though on the surface it seemed they kept in

close contact, the truth was they were never *with* each other.

It was for the best, she told herself. Less chance for her emotions to run away with her. Less chance that she might in some way reveal her love for him.

Besides which, her vanity was involved. She was huge and clumsy and felt unattractive. She had forgotten what it was like to be able to see her toes, and these days it took her twice the time to do the simplest task. But she was managing as well as could be expected, she reflected. As well as could be expected, that is, for a two-ton elephant.

Either Conall's housekeeper, cook, or his factotum, Robert—all three very nice people—were always in the house with her. And she kept occupied, reading, seeing movies, shopping, knitting, walking. And sometimes she would simply sit in the rocking chair by her bedroom window, stare out at the sky, and marvel over the life that was growing inside her. Her most fervent wish was coming true. She was going to have a baby.

There was another wish, however, another yearning that troubled her greatly.

When she had first realized she still loved Conall, she had had to acknowledge that the love was an impossibility. And so she had made the painful decision to leave him and SwanSea and get on with her life. At the time she had thought she would be able to tuck her love for him away in some corner of her heart, rather like tucking a box of old letters in the top of a closet. She would know where it was and she could take the box down every so often to savor its contents, then return it to the shelf until the next time.

But once again a plan of hers wasn't working.

*   *   *

Sharon glanced at the clock on the table beside her. Midnight. She made a sound of disgust. She was really fighting the idea of going to bed tonight. But then, there was no use lying in bed, miserable, when she could be just as miserable sitting on the couch, reading.

Besides, as her pregnancy had advanced and the time drew nearer for her delivery, her nightmares about going to the hospital had become steadily worse. In the darkness of her sleep, the blood was a brilliant, vivid red color, and the pain like multiple stab wounds. It had reached the point where she'd rather stay awake than risk the mental suffering that would come with her dreams.

She made an attempt to settle herself more comfortably against the pillows that she'd arranged in a corner of the couch and went back to her book. Five minutes later, when she heard the knock at her door, she realized she was still on the same page.

"Come in," she called, and waited expectantly for Conall to enter. Sometimes if he came home late and saw her light on beneath her door, he would stop to see how she was doing. And she had the sudden awful thought that maybe she had been subconsciously hoping to see him tonight and that was why she had delayed making her way to the bed.

The door opened, Conall walked in, and her heart leapt. Being nine months pregnant, she thought ruefully, didn't keep her from responding with love and desire at the sight of him.

"Why aren't you asleep?" he asked, crossing the room and sinking down into the opposite corner of the couch.

"I know it's late, but I was really enjoying the book—" A tiny foot jabbed her in her stomach as if in rebuke for telling the white lie. Her hand dropped to the huge mound. "And," she added, her tone wry as this time she told a portion of the truth, "I'm having trouble getting comfortable."

"Is the baby more active than usual tonight?"

"Definitely. And his exercise periods seem to get longer and more strenuous with each passing day." She had noticed that Conall rarely referred directly to the baby, concentrating instead on her and her physical condition.

She had noticed something else too. The baby seemed to become unusually energetic whenever Conall was near, or sometimes even when he was just on the phone with her. Was it possible, she wondered, that the baby felt his father's presence? No, she decided. More than likely the baby was simply responding to her accelerated pulse rate.

"Maybe he or she is getting eager to come out and see what the world is all about."

"I think it's going to be a he," she said on impulse, and watched for a reaction. The polite, reserved mask he wore never slipped.

"Really? Why?"

"Just a feeling. When I talk to him, I seem to hear a little boy's voice."

"What does he say?"

She looked closely at him but could detect only casual interest. They were strangers, she thought. Strangers who had conceived a child—exactly as she had wanted. "Actually he reassures me a lot."

"About what?"

She had said more than she should, had revealed too much. "Oh, things like he'll never scare me with spiders or frogs. That sort of thing."

He nodded as if he believed her. Or as if it weren't important to him whether or not she was telling the truth.

"Are you afraid of spiders and frogs?"

"I suppose I'll learn to cope. Mothers do, I understand."

"How much longer do you have? Two weeks?"

"About that. The doctor says you never know with first babies."

"I'm sure you're eager to have it all over with."

"Yes. I'm excited about the baby, but . . ." Her voice trailed off as suddenly the specter of the hospital appeared and froze her to the bone.

"But what?"

"Nothing. Are you just getting home from work?"

"Yes. Now I've answered your question. You answer mine. What's wrong?"

"I said nothing."

Surprising her, he slid across the couch until he was closer to her. "Sharon, don't you think I've noticed the shadows that have reappeared beneath your eyes? They're exactly like the ones I saw when I found you in San Diego."

"No—"

"Yes," he said, gently contradicting her. "Now, I know you get up early and that you exercise. It seems to me you should be able to sleep, even with the discomfort of the baby."

"Is that your diagnosis, doctor?" she asked, somewhat disconcerted to learn that he had been paying such close attention to her without her realizing it.

"All right, so I don't know what I'm talking about. But I do know what I can see with my own two eyes. You're not sleeping. I don't suppose you'd care to tell me why?"

"No."

"Okay." He stretched his arm along the back of the couch until it lay behind her.

The baby kicked. She eyed Conall nervously. "What are you doing?"

"I'm not sure. I guess I'm trying to figure out if you're really all right."

She racked her brain for something she could tell him. "The doctor says—"

"I don't want to hear what the doctor says. I want to hear what you say."

She rubbed the side of her face, then dropped her hand back to her stomach. He wasn't going to give up until she gave him a plausible explanation he would believe. She tried to think of one, but her mind was alarmingly blank. In the end she blurted out the truth. "I've been having nightmares."

"About what?" he asked, concern heavy in his voice.

"Going to the hospital. The idea terrifies me."

"But why? The hospital you will be going to is one of the finest in the country. I'm on the board of directors, and I can assure you that both you and the baby will be getting the very best of care."

"I know you're right." She glanced vaguely around the room, trying to find something on which she could focus and concentrate. Ultimately, her gaze returned to Conall. "It's the same hospital."

"The same hospital as what?"

She swallowed. "The same hospital I went to when I had the miscarriage."

"Oh, my Lord." His hand came off the back of the sofa to grip her shoulder. "I'm sorry, Sharon. It never once occurred to me that you'd still have bad memories of the place."

"It's silly, isn't it? I mean, I know I shouldn't be scared, but—" Her voice broke, and before she knew what he was doing, Conall gathered her close against him, huge stomach and all.

It had been so long since his arms had been around her, she wanted to close her eyes and soak up the sensations that came with being held by him. But now that she had started telling him of her nightmare, both waking and sleeping, she couldn't seem to stop.

"I can still remember how cold I was," she murmured, her face pressed against his chest. "Someone put a blanket over me, but I couldn't stop shaking. A doctor had seen me and told me I was losing the baby and that I would have to be taken into surgery. Emergency was busy that night, and they didn't have enough examining rooms for everyone, so they wheeled me out into a hall to wait until someone from surgery came for me. I don't know how long I waited. But I remember people hurrying by me as if they didn't see me, as if I didn't exist."

She was vaguely aware that she had begun to cry.

"It was the loneliest, most wretched feeling in the world. And then there was the pain and the blood and the cold."

"I'm sorry," he whispered, beginning a slight rocking motion with his body, comforting her as if she were a small child.

"And everything was so white. There was no color. Except for the blood. And there was no one who would hold my hand, call me by my name, and tell me everything would be all right, no one to care or even stop beside me, except the man who came to wheel me to surgery."

He rocked her until she quieted. Then he lifted her into his arms and carried her to the bed. There, he took off his shoes, jacket, and tie, climbed in beside her, and held her until morning.

And that night there were no nightmares.

When Sharon came down for dinner the next evening, she was surprised to see Conall sitting at the dining room table. "I didn't expect you to be here."

"I was able to break away early today," he said, rising to pull out a chair for her.

As he pushed the chair in, he leaned over her, and she felt a rolling sensation in her stomach, then a tiny fist.

As he returned to his seat, she unfolded her napkin and placed it in her lap. "I owe you an apology, Conall."

He looked over at her. "Not that I'm aware of."

"Yes, yes, I do. I should never have burdened you with my worries like I did last night."

"I told you I'd be there for you when you need me, and I will. That's a promise I won't break."

She nodded and made an attempt at a light laugh. "I appreciate that, especially since this fear of mine is so foolish."

He reached across the table for her hand. "I don't think it's foolish at all, and what's more, I understand completely."

"You do?"

"Yes," he said, "and I'm going to make you another promise. When you go to the hospital this time, you won't be afraid."

"How can you promise me that?"

"Because I won't let you be afraid." He smiled at her expression of doubt. "I thought you believed a Deverell could do anything."

"Yes, well . . ."

He squeezed her hand. "Trust me."

She still wasn't sure she could, but there was one more thing he needed to know. "I was told earlier, and now it's been confirmed by my doctor here. It appears that the birth canal is too narrow and the delivery will likely be by cesarean."

His expression darkened, but his voice remained calm and reassuring. "I will be with you, Sharon. I won't leave you. You can depend on me."

She nodded, choosing not to share her doubts with him.

The conversation turned casual, and for Sharon, the evening passed enjoyably. At bedtime they parted, she going to her room, Conall to his.

But later, after she'd been asleep for several hours, the nightmares came again. She awoke shaking and in a cold sweat.

Without thinking through what she was going to do, she slipped out of bed, left her room, and hurried down the hall.

Conall heard his bedroom door open and switched on his bedside light to see Sharon. Her face was white, her lips colorless, and even with the distance that separated them, he could see that she was shaking.

"What's wrong?" he asked, alarmed, sitting up. "Are you all right?"

"Yes, yes. It's just that I had another bad dream, and I was wondering . . ."

He pulled back the covers and slid over to give her room.

With a sigh of relief she crossed the room and climbed into bed beside him. She was so big, it took her a minute to get comfortably positioned, but finally she was settled, as close as possible to Conall without touching him. Lying on sheets already warmed by him, near enough to him to feel his body heat, she was content. And she slept without nightmares.

The next night, without any discussion of the matter, Conall waited until she had had time to get ready for bed, then went and got her and took her to his room.

That night and those that followed, with him lying beside her, she slept peacefully and dreamed only of him.

She hurt, she thought vaguely. Bands of pain were wrapped around her, gripping her so tightly she could scarcely breathe. If she could only wake herself up, get out of this dream.

"Sharon, what's wrong?"

She heard Conall's voice, felt his hand on her shoulder.

"What's wrong, Sharon? Are you having a dream?"

She tried to tell him yes, but she was too tangled up in the nightmare. She moaned as another pain racked her body. Any minute now she'd see the blood, feel the cold.

"Wake up, sweetheart. I'm here. I won't let anything bad happen to you."

Sweetheart. He had called her sweetheart. She waited until the pain had subsided, rolled carefully over onto her back, and forced her eyes open.

"Are you all right?" he asked.

She saw his face in the light from the bedside lamp, worried and anxious. "I don't know. I think . . ." She gasped as pain gripped her again. Instinctively she put her hand over her stomach. It was rigid. When she could talk again, she said, "I don't think this is a dream. I think I'm in labor . . . I think I have been for quite a while."

Panic seized him, but he was careful not to let what he was feeling show. He reached for the phone and punched in the number of Robert's room. Next he called the doctor.

Both conversations were brief, and when he hung up, he turned back to Sharon. He took her hand and held it against his heart. "Everything's going to be all right. Do you believe me?"

Strangely enough, she did. "Yes."

"Good, then let's go."

He helped her into her robe and slippers, then stripped the comforter off the bed and wrapped her in it. As if her weight were nothing, he lifted her and carried her downstairs and into the waiting car. Robert drove, and Conall sat in the backseat with her, cradling her against him. Whenever a contraction struck, he would press his lips against her forehead and murmur encouragingly to her.

She listened closely to him, drawing comfort from both his words and the gentleness of his voice. At one point she heard him tell Robert to use the car phone to call the hospital and remind them they would be arriving by the front door. She wanted to tell him that they were supposed to go through the emergency entrance, but at that moment she had another contraction.

She hadn't taken any type of childbirth classes because she hadn't wanted to ask Conall to be her partner. He was already so busy, she had told herself, but the truth was she didn't feel emotionally up to the task of working that closely with him. She had worried that in some way she might expose her true feelings for him. Now she wished she had taken the risk. But even though she hadn't had the classes, she had read every book she could lay her hands on and knew to pant during the contractions.

The short, quick breaths helped, but her greatest consolation came from Conall's nearness.

The trip to the hospital seemed relatively short, but by the time they arrived, her pain was mixed with an incredible pressure.

Two attendants, a nurse, and a resident were waiting at curbside with a gurney. But Conall was the one who lifted her onto the stretcher and adjusted the comforter around her. And he was the one who walked beside her, never once letting go of her hand.

She focused on his touch, his voice. When he told her to close her eyes so that the bright lights of the hospital wouldn't hurt, she did. When he told her to hang on, that this would soon be over, she believed him. When he told someone in a voice that brooked no argument that he was going into the operating room with her, she was extremely thankful.

During the short time he was gone to scrub up and don a gown and mask, a nurse with soft hands and a soothing voice called her by name, stroked her forehead, and told her how brave she was. Sharon didn't believe her, but when Conall returned and told her the same thing, she knew it was true.

She held tightly to his hand and drew strength from the warmth of his eyes. Then very quickly she grew drowsy and her lids became too heavy to lift.

But she still had Conall's voice to give her strength. And soon she had a baby son in her arms.

She awoke in a room that was bursting with vivid red, blue, green, and every other color of the rainbow. She squeezed her eyes shut, then opened them again. Bouquets of balloons floated close to the ceiling. Arrangements of flowers were on every available surface and around the baseboard of the room. Stained glass birds of all kinds hung at the windows, reflecting bright, joyous, colored light. She felt as if she had been transported to a magical wonderland while she had slept.

"Hi."

The sound of Conall's voice drew her head around. "Hi." Her tongue flicked over her lips to moisten the dryness. "Where am I?"

He poured water from a pitcher into a glass. "You're in your room at the hospital."

"Really?" Her tone was soft with amazement. Then, "*The baby!*"

"He's fine."

He slid his hand through her hair and lifted her head so that she could sip the water.

"I remember seeing him last night," she said when she was again lying on the pillow. "He was tiny and wrinkled, but he was wonderful. Have you seen him since we were in the delivery room?"

He nodded. "He's still wrinkled, but he's blessedly healthy, and he cries louder than any other baby in the nursery."

"He's crying? Why is he crying?"

"I asked the same thing and was assured it was perfectly normal."

"Who assured you?"

"Two different doctors."

Sharon studied him. There had been a surprising lack of emotion in his face and voice as he had spoken of the baby. On the other hand, it had taken two doctors to assure him that it was normal for his baby to cry. She was a bit groggy, but she had the feeling there was something important here she was missing and should be getting.

Then she noticed his appearance. He was in his shirtsleeves, his eyes shadowed with fatigue, his jaws darkened by an overnight growth of beard.

"When can I see the baby?"

"They said they would bring him in as soon as you think you're alert enough. They've given you something for pain."

"I guess that accounts for my grogginess."

"Would you like to sit up a little?"

"Yes, please."

He pushed a button on a control unit. The head of the bed slowly rose, and as it did, she noticed a plump blue chenille elephant sitting at the bottom of the bed, and a tall yellow and brown giraffe standing in one corner of the room.

"Did you do all this?" she asked.

"Well, I happened to be passing the gift shop—"

Her mind wasn't that fogged. "When?"

"When?"

"You haven't left my side, have you? There was no gift shop."

"Actually, there's one downstairs."

"You arranged for all of this days ago, didn't you?"

"Well . . ."

"Thank you, Conall."

"For what?"

"You kept your promise. You were with me every step of the way. I never once felt alone or cold or afraid. I can't thank you enough."

He took her hand, and for a heart-stopping moment their eyes met and held. For an instant she could have sworn she saw a shading of vulnerability in the cobalt-blue depths. Then he was releasing her hand.

"You're welcome," he said briskly. "Would you like me to ask a nurse to come in and help you freshen up?"

"That would be nice. Then I want to see my baby."

"Good. I'm glad you feel up to it." Conall rose and started for the door.

For some reason she panicked. "Wait."

He stopped, rested his hands on the rails of her bed, and gazed down at her.

"You're coming back, aren't you?" she asked.

"I thought I'd run home and change."

"But then you'll come back, won't you? You could see the baby," she added as a temptation to him.

"I'll come back if you want me to."

"I do."

He hesitated. "They'll be asking you about a name for the baby soon. Do you have any in mind?"

"Actually I had been thinking about Clarisse if it was a girl and Jacob if it was a boy."

"And now that you know the baby is a boy?"

"I like Jacob, and I think it's fitting."

Pleasure briefly lightened his face, then was gone. "And what about a last name?"

"Graham," she said, vaguely amazed he should ask.

He nodded. "I'll send the nurse in."

Conall had had Sharon and Jacob home just a few days before he began to worry, and by the end of four weeks he was positively frantic. She was feeling stronger with every passing day, and he knew as soon as she was fully recovered, she'd be eager to leave.

And when that time came, he didn't know how he'd be able to go on living.

He was doing everything in his power to keep her from getting nervous about his intentions toward the baby. But it was so hard to keep his emotions neutral and not allow any of what he was feeling to show. Whenever he saw that little boy, his heart melted. He'd never known anything so tiny could be that precious and sweet, even fascinating. He wanted to shout it from the roof-tops that he had become the father of the most wonderful baby in the whole world. He wanted to hold him, to talk to him, to make plans for him. He wanted to buy his son every toy in the world. But he didn't do any of those things.

If Sharon caught so much as a glimpse of what he was feeling, he'd never make her believe he'd loved her and had been searching for her before he'd learned she was pregnant.

He was trying to be so careful with her, not pressure her in any way. But he made up his mind. He wasn't going to let her go without a fight.

He'd come up with an idea that might keep her with him a little longer and give him the time he needed to convince her to stay with him always. He just hoped she would go for his idea.

"SwanSea?" Sharon said a few days later, cast-ing a glance at Jacob, who was sleeping content-edly in his cradle nearby. "You want us to go to SwanSea?"

"I can guarantee that the trip will be very easy on both you and Jacob, and of course we'll check with the doctor before we leave. I think you'll be able to recuperate better there. Fewer interrup-tions, staff at your fingertips, that sort of thing."

"But I have all of that here."

"Yes, but I still think SwanSea would be better for you, the baby—for the three of us. After all, that's where Jacob was conceived. I think it's appropriate that he at least see it before . . ." He trailed off, furious with himself for even suggesting that there might be a time when she would leave. "And the truth of the matter is, I could use the rest."

Now, there was a reason that made sense to her. Lately he had been looking drawn and pale, and she was worried about him. There had been times when she wondered if having Jacob and her living in his house was getting on his nerves. But here he was, suggesting that they all three travel to SwanSea together. She'd be a fool not to jump at the opportunity, she decided. She didn't know how much time she had left with him.

"I think you're right," she said. "It's a good idea. Let's go."

"I'll make the arrangements. Oh, and I have something for you." He handed her a small package he'd managed to keep out of sight.

"A present?" she asked, excited. "Is it for Jacob?"

"No, it's for you."

She cast him an astonished glance, but then quickly unwrapped the box, lifted the lid, and pulled out a Hummel figurine. It was of a small, apple-cheeked boy and a frog, curiously surveying each other.

She grinned. "I love it."

"I know Jacob promised you he wouldn't scare you with spiders and frogs, but I have a feeling it won't stop him from playing with them."

"I'm sure you're right." A warmth welled inside her at his thoughtfulness, but she wasn't quite sure how to put what she was feeling into words, so she said what was in her heart. "Thank you."

"You're welcome," he said softly.

Ten

As the car carrying Sharon, Conall, and Jacob swept up the drive, Sharon leaned forward in her seat to better view the great house that had made such a vivid and unusual impression on her during her previous visit.

The sky was a brilliant, cloudless blue, the wind only a whisper. It gently stirred the tops of flowers on the verge of exploding with color in celebration of the beginning of summer.

And commanding the entire scene, SwanSea stood magnificent and proud beneath the light from a radiant sun. Looking closely, it seemed to Sharon as if the great house were shimmering with an eagerness and an anticipation.

Remembering how angry SwanSea had seemed as she had driven away that stormy, early morning so many months before, she wondered if the house had somehow known what she herself had not—that she was pregnant with a Deverell baby. She shook her head slightly as if to physically rid herself of that preposterous notion.

"Oh, no," Conall muttered. "I swear, Sharon, I had nothing to do with this."

"What is it?" she asked, then she saw for herself. All available staff were lined along the drive. And at the head of the line, beaming in a most dignified way, was Winston Lawrence. She groaned. "This is all in honor of Jacob. Who told them?"

"I suppose I have to take the blame," he said, sounding anything but guilty. "I called and requested a cradle for him. We could have made him a bed in a bureau drawer, but I don't know how long we could have hidden his presence from them. Maids, bellboys, room service . . ."

The car rolled to a stop, and she plastered a smile on her face for all those peering into the car. "You're right, I guess. And as long as they don't call him the young master, I'll be all right."

"Good girl." He opened the door on his side, climbed out, and walked around the car to open her door. She didn't offer to relinquish her sleeping son to him, and he didn't ask. With a hand on her arm, he helped her out.

Winston Lawrence stepped forward. "We are so pleased and honored to have you back with us, Ms. Graham. And I can't tell you how excited we are to also have young master Jacob with us. It's a great day, a great day indeed."

Conall choked back a laugh, and Sharon shot him a look, playfully murderous.

"Young Jacob's great-grandfather would be so proud," the manager went on to say, oblivious to their byplay.

"Thank you," Sharon murmured. "I appreciate everyone turning out to greet us, but I wonder if we might go on up to our rooms. The trip and all . . ." She trailed off vaguely.

"But of course. Immediately. Peter, William, Jennifer."

Three young people sprang into action, and minutes later she was in the suite she and Conall had occupied before, her bags in the room in which she had spent exactly one night, his bags in the other. She assumed the instructions as to where to put the bags had come from Conall, as had the order for the waist-high cradle heavily inlaid with mother-of-pearl.

"Are you okay?" Conall asked sometime later as he strolled into the sitting room and found her on the couch. Everyone else had left and she had put Jacob down to continue his nap.

"I'm fine."

"Listen, if their slightly proprietary attitude—"

"Slightly?"

"—bothers you," he finished, grinning, 'I'll put an end to it."

"No, no. They mean well. And if they get on my nerves, I have an ace up my sleeve."

To her delight, he gasped in alarm. "You don't mean—"

She nodded solemnly. "Yes, I do mean. I'll order a bowl of chocolate chip ice cream without the chocolate chips."

His laughter rang through the room and made her heart beat faster than was good for her emotional well-being. But she seized and hung on to this uncomplicated time with him because she knew it would soon be coming to an end.

As the days turned into a week and then another week, her body healed and her reason and resolve regarding her relationship with Conall began to unravel. Suddenly she couldn't seem to make her plans come into as sharp a focus as she had before. A lethargy had invaded her system that kept her delaying the time when she would take Jacob and move back to her little house in San Diego. She blamed it all on the fact that her hormones were still skewed from Jacob's birth.

But to further muddy the waters of her thought processes, a new element had entered their relationship. On the surface Conall did nothing differently. He took care of her as no one had ever done before, making sure she and the baby had everything they needed. And he had a way of being there beside her before she had a chance to get lonely or depressed.

But she sensed an inner tension in him. Every once in a while she would glance up to find him watching her. It was as if he were waiting for something to happen, and she couldn't help but wonder if he was waiting for her to leave.

Then one day she happened to walk into her room and see him leaning over the cradle, gazing at his sleeping son. The hunger and yearning she saw on his face brought her up short and made her realize she had been walking around blind.

She had been selfishly stretching her time with Conall, not understanding that the longer she stayed, the more time he had to become attached to his son.

His air of detachment had fooled her into thinking that he didn't care for the baby, wouldn't want him. Now she realized just how wrong she had been. His act of detachment had been a defense mechanism to protect him from being hurt.

She felt as if she were being torn in two. Her love for him had grown deeper with Jacob's birth, and there was no doubt in her mind that Conall would make a wonderful father. But it would mess up all three of them if she stayed with the man because he wanted the child. No, she had to leave. And soon.

She backed out of the room before he saw her

and went for a long walk along the cliffs. She understood now what she had to do. All that was left was to decide how best to broach the subject of her leaving to Conall, and then the hardest part, how to find the courage to make herself carry through.

She stood on the cliff top and looked out at the rolling sea. She considered herself strong, but leaving Conall was going to call for a strength she wasn't sure she possessed, she wasn't even sure existed.

All at once a movement down on the beach caught her attention.

A tall, lean man with sandy-colored hair rode a palomino along the water's edge, a man who once seen could never be mistaken for anyone else. Amarillo Smith.

Sharon mentioned seeing him to Conall that night while they were having dinner in their suite.

"Really? I didn't know Rill was here, but I'm not surprised. Like me, he keeps horses here, and whenever possible he comes up for a day or two. He'll be staying here on the fourth floor with us. I'll have to look him up and say hello."

"Do you think he's here alone?"

"I've never known him to bring anyone with him. He and Nico are as close as brothers and I consider him my friend, but basically he's very much a loner. Occasionally he'll bring a woman to one function or another, but only when it's convenient or he's in the mood."

"Oh." She pushed a pea around her plate with her fork.

"Is something on your mind?" Conall asked. "You've seemed preoccupied all afternoon. Don't you feel well?"

In spite of, or maybe because of the sadness

inside her, she smiled. "Did anyone ever tell you that you are a born nurturer?"

"A what?"

"Someone who nurtures others."

He took a sip of wine. "You're kidding, right?"

"No, I'm not. You probably never had anyone to take care of before, because all the Deverells are so self-sufficient. But then I came along"—she grimaced—"a clinically perfect case of someone who needed to be taken care of."

"I told you I'd be there for you."

"And you have been. It's been a long time since I've had anyone I could lean on unconditionally. Maybe I *never* had anyone, I don't know." She paused, trying to gather her thoughts, her resolve. "But I've been able to lean on you these last few months, and you'll never know how much I appreciate it."

Realizing what was coming, Conall went still. He'd dreaded this moment, deliberately avoiding the confrontation because he hadn't wanted to risk losing their tenuous peace before it was necessary. But now that the moment had come, he looked forward to it. Bringing everything out in the open would end this hellish limbo in which he'd been holding himself. "I don't want your gratitude, Sharon."

"Nevertheless you have it."

He waited, just as he had been ever since Jacob had been born.

"Conall, I think it's time Jacob and I leave."

"Do you?"

She nodded. "We've disrupted your life enough. It's time we left so that you can get on with your life and we can get on with ours."

"That's what you think, is it?"

She finally noticed the unusual control in his voice, the tension in his body. "Don't you?"

"No."

She stared at him uncertainly.

Conall rested his forearms on the table and leaned toward her. "Sharon, I want you to spend the rest of your life with me. I want you to marry me."

"M-marry you?" She felt so stupid, because for some reason a proposal was the last thing she had expected. But it made perfect sense. He wanted Jacob.

"I don't expect you to believe me, but I love you."

She swallowed against a dry throat, acutely aware how extremely painful it was to be offered what you wanted more than anything in the world when you were offered it for the wrong reasons. "You're right. I find that hard to believe."

"I don't know how to convince you either."

"Try to understand, Conall. You've been wonderful to me during these past months. But there was a time you weren't so wonderful, a time when you turned your back. Consequently, it's hard for me to forget that this new concern and care of yours has all been just since you found out I was pregnant. And now Jacob is here, and you're a man who has everything but a son."

"And you. I don't have you, Sharon."

She wanted more than anything to be able to trust what she was hearing, but she couldn't. "You're just saying that because you know that to get Jacob you'd have to take me."

"That's not true."

"You can't have Jacob alone."

He grimaced. "That wasn't what I meant. I promised you I wouldn't take your baby away from you, and I won't. What I meant was that I have only one reason for asking you to marry me, and that is because I love you. Actually I realized

I loved you before I received the doctor's medical report."

Her skepticism was blatant. "Then why didn't you tell me before now?"

"You were in no shape, emotionally, to hear this either when I found you or after Jacob was born. He saw her draw a breath to speak, but he forestalled her by rushing on. "It's true I would love to have the opportunity to be Jacob's full-time father. It's also true that I loved him the moment I saw him. But I wouldn't ask you to marry me if first and foremost I didn't love you. I simply wouldn't do that to either of us."

His logic was wearing her down, and she kept telling herself that she should know better than to weaken. She had to come up with some sort of defense. Slowly, she straightened. "But what if it's *me* that wouldn't do that to either of us."

"What do you mean?"

"What if I don't love you?"

He thought he heard the sound of his heart breaking in two. He certainly felt the pain of it. Leaning back in his chair, he gazed steadily at her. *This* was the real reason he had put off asking her to marry him for as long as he had, he realized. He hadn't wanted to hear her say she didn't love him, hadn't wanted to hear that final no.

"I don't have the answer to that question," he said at last. "I can only see this from my point of view, how much I love you, how much I want you, how much I want you, me, and Jacob to be a family."

"But—"

He lifted his hand, about to try what would surely be almost impossible for him—putting all the hope and love he felt into a dry, emotionless form. "Hear me out. It seems to me that we have all the ingredients for a good relationship. When we were here together before, the sex was explosive. Without the sex, we get along well and we have fun together. We both love and want the best for Jacob. Having said that, I guess it's up to you to decide whether or not that's enough for you to commit to a lifelong relationship. And please note, I said lifelong. Once we're married, we'll stay married."

He made the issues she needed to face sound so simple, but their relationship had always been tangled and involved. "I—I need time to think."

"Of course. Just don't take too much time." He might fall apart completely if she kept him waiting too long.

SwanSea was brooding again. Sharon sat on the rise behind the great house and stared down at it. Either that or she was going crazy, and she had to admit that it was more than likely the latter.

It was early afternoon of the day after Conall had asked her to marry him. Her brain hurt, she had been thinking so much, and she had badly needed to get out of the suite. Conall had gone for a swim, so she had fed Jacob, gathered a few of his things plus a quilt into a bag, and strapped on a baby carrier that allowed her to carry him against her heart. Now he lay beside her, cooing and gurgling in the sun.

And SwanSea was brooding because she was thinking of taking him away again.

She sighed. Crazy, that's what she was. But she'd just have to get over it because Jacob needed and deserved a sane mother.

But what about a father? a small voice in her hurting head asked.

Good question.

It all came down to whether she believed Conall. He said he wanted her, but her fear was that it was really the baby he wanted. She just couldn't be sure he would still want her if she didn't have Jacob. She sighed.

Last night when he had asked her to marry him, she had flung his actions of ten years before in his face. But she knew she had grown and changed in the last ten years. Why was she so reluctant to think he had?

Right from the start he had been truthful with her. He had kept each of his promises, and he had treated her with a gentleness and a caring—more so in fact than she had had any right to expect under the circumstances.

And having covered that ground, she squarely faced several facts from which she could not escape. She loved him. She did trust him. She definitely wanted to spend the rest of her life with him.

After all the agonizing, all the doubting, all the hurting, could it really be that simple? It seemed it was.

She smiled down at Jacob, who was wildly swinging his arms. "Guess what? I'm going to marry your father. Want to give me away?"

Jacob looked up at her with his dark blue eyes, gurgled happily, then kicked.

"I guess that means I have your approval," she said softly.

The sudden sound of horse hooves brought her head around and she saw Amarillo approaching. She had mixed emotions about him. There was a part of her that instinctively resented the fact that he had hunted her down, tracking her like some wild animal with a patience and diligence that was frightening. But then there was another part of her—a very large part of her—that was extremely glad he had found her.

He reined in his horse on the side of her opposite from Jacob and several yards away, but with a mother's nervousness Sharon picked up her baby and held him.

He nodded to her. "Enjoying the sun?"

"Yes, thank you. And you?"

"Yes, but I'm heading back to Boston this afternoon, so I'm glad I got the opportunity to see you before I left."

"Oh?"

"I've already told Conall, but I'd like you to know also that it's been good to see you two together here."

She started to inform him that they hadn't been together, not exactly, at least not yet, but he went on.

"He was an absolute wreck when you disappeared. I don't think I've ever seen a man so in love with a woman." He paused, and there was the faintest twinkle in his eye. "Well, maybe with the small exception of Nico. But at any rate, Conall was in pretty bad shape, and then when that medical report came—"

"You mean you thought he was in love with me before the medical report came?"

"There was no thinking about it. He *was*. But now you're together and you have Jacob." As if he had said it all with his last sentence, he lifted a hand in good-bye. "I'll be seeing you."

As he wheeled his horse and trotted away, Sharon looked after him. He had just validated the decision she had come to on her own. It was nice to have proof that she had been right. But she was extremely thankful she had arrived at her decision without Amarillo's proof.

* * *

Conall swung around as the door to the sitting room opened. "Sharon! Where in the hell have you been?"

His obvious agitation caught her off guard and brought her back to the earth she had mentally left the moment she had made her decision. All the way back to the house she'd been practically bursting with joy, and she was sure her feet hadn't touched the ground once.

Now she eyed the pallor beneath the bronze hue of his skin with concern. "I took Jacob out for some sun. Have you been worried?"

"Worried." He bit off the word with a curse. "I came back from the pool to find both you and Jacob gone, and it was like reliving that morning when I woke up and you had vanished."

She reached out and touched his arm. "Conall, I'm so sorry. I would have left you a note, but it never occurred to me that you would think something like that."

"Sharon, we've got to talk."

"You're right, we do. I have something to tell you. Just let me put Jacob down. All that sun and fresh air has put him to sleep."

"Wait," he said as she started into the bedroom. He walked over to her, leaned down, and tenderly kissed his son's soft head.

Jacob opened his tiny eyes and gazed up at his father. To Sharon's amazement, it appeared as if he smiled at Conall. Then he closed his eyes and promptly fell asleep again.

"It won't take me long," she murmured, touched by the kiss and the smile but confused by the defiant look Conall cast her. Minutes later when she returned, she found him standing by one of the open French doors, staring out at the sea. He swung around.

"Conall—" she began.

"No, Sharon. I've got to speak first."

"All right," she said slowly, an uneasy feeling beginning in her that he might have changed his mind.

"Sharon, last night when I asked you to marry me, I pretty much laid all my cards on the table. When I did, I told myself that I'd done everything I could, and that if in the end you decided to move back to San Diego, I'd just have to accept it. Well, maybe that's what I should do, but I can't. I realized that today when I came in here, and for a short awful time I thought you'd gone again."

Relief swept through her. "Oh, Conall, please don't say anything else. Just listen." Distressed she had hurt him, she couldn't wait a moment longer to tell him of her decision. He had suffered enough. They both had.

His expression turned fierce, and he took her arms in an urgent grip. "No, *you* listen. You've got to marry me, Sharon. Because if you don't, I won't make it. Say you'll marry me. Tell me you love me."

"I do love you," she said softly. "And I will marry you and stay with you—always and forever."

"Are you sure?"

"Yes. It's what I've been trying to tell you. If I can possibly help it, I won't ever lose you again."

With a hard shudder he pulled her to him in a crushing embrace. "Thank God," he muttered, then kissed her deeply, lovingly. She slid her hands around his waist, and when he finally lifted his head, he saw a love shining from her that was pure and radiant and strong. Emotion overcame him, and he blinked away a tear.

"We have your grandfather, Jake, to thank for

this," she murmured. "If I hadn't received his note of promise to Clarisse, I would never have come to you."

"I agree," he said hoarsely. "I will always be grateful to him. And to you for having the courage to come to me."

"His gift of love redeemed our lost love."

"And this is my promise to you," he whispered, brushing a sweetly curling strand of hair from her face. "I will love you until the day I die and after."

Tears of happiness filled her eyes and clung to her lashes as he swept her into his arms and carried her into his bedroom, careful to leave the door ajar in case their son awakened.

Outside, the sun shone down on SwanSea, warming its stone walls to a golden hue, glinting off its windows so that they sparkled, giving a beatific appearance to the great house.

A new Deverell slept within its walls. In a short while the house would fill with Deverells to meet and celebrate the newest of them.

The years would pass, the child would grow to become a man, the man would father a child. And there would be another child to protect and watch over. The legacy would continue.

For now, SwanSea was content.